MW00974344

Copyright © 2018 Disney Enterprises, Inc.

All rights reserved. Published by Disney Press, an imprint of Disney Book Group.

No part of this book may be reproduced or transmitted in any form or by any means, electronic or mechanical, including photocopying, recording, or by any information storage and retrieval system, without written permission from the publisher. For information address Disney Press, 1200 Grand Central Avenue, Glendale, California 91201.

Printed in the United States of America

First Hardcover Edition, July 2018

10 9 8 7 6 5 4 3 2 1

FAC-038091-18166

ISBN 978-1-368-02432-7

For more Disney Press fun, visit www.disneybooks.com

SUSTAINABLE FORESTRY INITIATIVE Certified Sourcing
www.sfiprogram.org
SFI-00993
Logo Applies to Text Stock Only

You've found this book hidden in my pirate ship, and you've dared to open its pages, so you're braver than most. But bravery won't get you far on the Isle of the Lost. You've got to be cunning, manipulative, and slippery as a wharf rock. You can't just _be_ a villain—you have to beat a villain at her own game.

I was born and raised on the Isle, daughter of a twice-banished sea witch. I know how to lie and steal and cheat my way through the days, barely stopping for a sword fight. But I'm not going to be here forever. I won't let myself waste away, trapped behind the barrier, Auradon mocking me in the distance. Before I make my escape, I figured I'd do something solid for all the villains I'm leaving behind. I won't forget about all the kids here on the Isle who look up to me, who don't have anyone else to boss them around or show them how to cheat the merchants on the wharf. Maybe life here is hard, but villains should help each other out however they can. You can do better than just survive here— you can _thrive_ here, and I'm not going to keep all that valuable info to myself. I'm not selfish like that traitor Mal, you know? How could I just take off and forget everyone still trapped behind the barrier?

To whoever finds this:

Here's everything you need to know about the Isle of the Lost. This is your guide to surviving, ruling, and escaping this wretched place. Everything I've learned is in these pages: tips and tricks and the things no one else will tell you. Because if you have to be on the Isle of the Lost, you should make the Isle of the Lost work for you, as long as you can possibly stand it.

Oh, and one last thing: GOOD LUCK.

—UMA

RULES of the ISLE

1 Quit your daydreams. Yeah, you can stare off beyond the barrier all day, wishing for something different, but that's not going to get you anywhere. Keep your head in the minute-by-minute and day-to-day.

2 Only tune in to that propaganda machine the Auradon News Network if you're studying it for a scheme. Too many hours of that nonsense and you'll be humming the Auradon Prep fight song in your sleep.

3

Isle of the Lost? More like Isle of the Lemmings. People here are desperate—for something to eat, for somewhere to go, for someone to follow. Be a leader and your minions will fall in line faster than you can say "pirate crew."

↑ MISERY LIVES HERE!

4 Hawk your wares. Everyone's got something to offer, so figure out how to profit from the Isle economy. Good at making snakeskin belts? Sell them by the wharf. Good at diving for forgotten treasure? Start a saltwater antiques business. Good at making shrimp-shell soup? Find something else to do—we already sell it at Ursula's Fish & chips shoppe.

~ 5 ~

Keep your friends close and your valuables closer. Everyone on the Isle is a freelance scammer, con artist, or pickpocket. An unattended bag is an invitation for villainy.

#6

watch out for falling seagull poop. seriously, those sky vermin are everywhere.

UNDER THE WEATHER

You can easily recognize the gloomy isle far out across the strait of Ursula. There's a dense, dark cloud that always hovers above the city, polluted with smoke from burnt garbage. I spent years staring up into that gray mess, hoping to get just a second of sunlight. No dice.

This is what no one will tell you: outwitting other villains and eating sea slop is easy compared to dealing with the weather on the Isle. Walking down the street every day, not knowing if it's ten in the morning or six at night? Awful. Time doesn't pass here the same way it passes everywhere else. It's a slow slog, day after day after gloomy day.

I cut this out of an old Auradon Prep history book that got dumped on the Isle. From the "Reign of Beast" section.

I guess "sunlight" was on the "things villains don't deserve" list, right after "freedom" and "magic." I hope Beast had a gleefully good time deciding our fate on that one. . . .

As for me? I tried to make the best of it. I tried to see it as an opportunity to toughen up. Hey, at least I never had to worry about sunglasses, sunblock, sunburn, or, you know, plants growing to their full height.

SEA VILLAIN

LOOK AT THE CHUM THAT
GOT CAUGHT IN THE NET!
   —HARRY

       Aw, thanks, chum!
            —GIL

     NOT HOW I MEANT IT!

He meant shark bait. <u>Not</u> "friend."
              Still works.

ISLE OF THE LEFTOVERS

One of the worst things about living on the Isle is getting charity from Beast and Belle. Every day there's some shipment from Auradon, all this secondhand stuff they've used and reused and then thrown away. Do they really think they're doing us a favor? How can the citizens of Auradon be proud of themselves for shipping over a boot with a hole in the toe? Or some old radio with a broken dial?

Well . . . I did find a cool bowling ball I've been using as a free weight. It has Fairy Godmother's name on the side in gold script. It's been keeping my biceps bulging.

Creamed Spinach

I'd rather eat goblin toe jam than use Fairy Godmother's old bowling ball. No way. Here are the worst things I've found in those piles of Auradon rubble:

- A jacket with a rip down the back (Beast definitely transformed too quickly and busted the seams on that one.)

- Two dozen cans of creamed spinach from Auradon Prep's cafeteria (two months expired, of course)

- A bag of fabric scraps from Evie's 4 Hearts business (Maybe some other girls on the Isle would want those, but I don't need to take charity from her.)

- Old glasses with a crack in one of the lenses

- Some beat-up jacket Carlos had (I wouldn't be caught dead in that ratty fur.)

COME ON, UMA. DON'T BE A SNOB. IT'S NOT ALL NASTY.
I'VE FOUND SOME GOOD LOOT OVER THE YEARS. . . .

BEST THINGS HARRY'S FOUND IN THE SHIPPING CRATES FROM AURADON

- GOLD LOCKET (I PAWNED IT AT JAFAR'S JUNK SHOP FOR A NEW WATCH.)

- CRACKED TIARA WITH TWO RUBIES STILL ON THE FRONT (YES, YOU READ THAT RIGHT: TWO RUBIES.)

- MAP OF AURADON CITY (I'M GOING TO USE IT WHEN I FINALLY GET OUT OF HERE.)

- A BAG OF TONGUE TINGLERS, THIS SOUR CANDY FROM AURADON THAT MAKES YOUR TONGUE NUMB. (I ATE ALL OF THEM IN A DAY.)

I do remember that. You couldn't speak for a week.

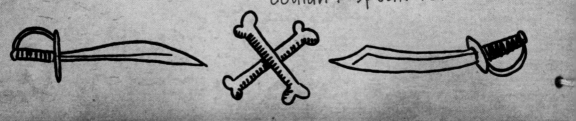

~~Remember when I found that old ball gown, Uma? The sparkly blue one? You used it to make that skirt you always wear.~~

I TOLD YOU NOT
TO REPEAT THAT, GIL.

I don't need people thinking I like deep-diving in Auradon bargain bins.

The LAY of the Land

There are so many places to go and things to see on the Isle of the Lost, and not all of them are good. Know your surroundings. Where to be (or not to be) is important, especially when danger lurks in every alley and abandoned shop. I've had my fair share of close calls: going down the wrong street on the wrong night when a band of pickpockets is lying in wait, or walking into **DUELS WITHOUT RULES** when there's an epic battle going on out back. Learn your lessons the easy way—by taking my word for things.

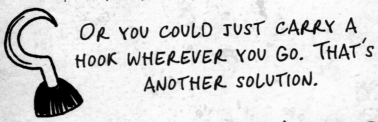

OR YOU COULD JUST CARRY A HOOK WHEREVER YOU GO. THAT'S ANOTHER SOLUTION.

SHUT IT, HARRY.

BARGAIN CASTLE

I hate to admit it, but my enemy's old pad is one of the biggest buildings on the Isle. It's right by the central market and in the middle of all the bazaar shops selling used clothes and boots. Now there's a store in the bottom of it that peddles enchanter robes and pointed hats.

Back in the day, before she got what she deserved (being shrunk into a garnish-sized lizard), Maleficent lived there with her daughter, Mal. They used to be so haughty, surveying the market from their balcony like they owned all the Isle. Since Mal's gone to Auradon, her old place is a disaster (and I don't mean that as a compliment). A bunch of ruffians raided it and took everything of value. There's a rumor Ginny Gothel, Mother Gothel's daughter, stole one of Maleficent's cloaks. There's also a rumor I was in there, too, hauling out armfuls of loot. I will neither confirm nor deny.

I'LL CONFIRM I WAS THERE. MALEFICENT HAD SOME GREAT STUFF, AND I EVEN NICKED HER BLACK NAIL POLISH.

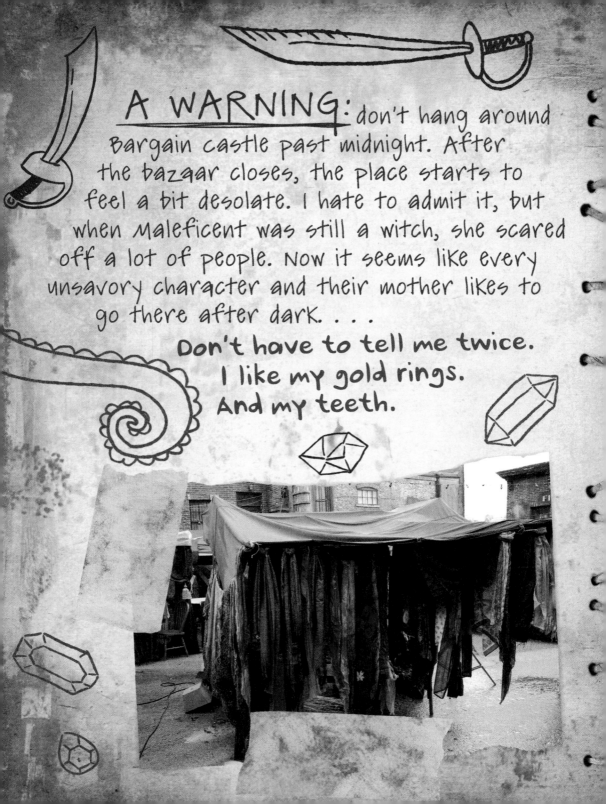

A WARNING: don't hang around

Bargain Castle past midnight. After the bazaar closes, the place starts to feel a bit desolate. I hate to admit it, but when Maleficent was still a witch, she scared off a lot of people. Now it seems like every unsavory character and their mother likes to go there after dark. . . .

Don't have to tell me twice.
I like my gold rings.
And my teeth.

JAFAR'S
JUNK SHOP

You almost feel bad for old Jafar, sitting around, counting his gold coins every day, watching his fortune dwindle as his boy yucks it up in Auradon. Jay was the one who used to run around nicking items to stock the shelves there. Now Jafar's shop is half empty.

You'll know the place because it's the one with two dozen locks on the front door. There've been too many break-ins to count. It's this crazy cycle on the Isle of the Lost: things are bought, nicked, bought again, nicked again . . . and it keeps going on and on like that. I've been in there a few times, slipping some of the smaller wares into my deep pockets. I've heard Jafar has a little room in the back with some sofas and rugs from Agrabah, but I've never seen it. Doubt he'll ever invite me back for tea . . .

FROLLO'S CREPERIE

All right, I know Claude Frollo is one of the vilest villains on the Isle of the Lost, but his crepes are legit. The place is dark and dank inside, and there are cobwebs in every corner and crevice, but that smell . . .

CHOCOLATE CREPES.

Savory cheese crepes. (So what if the cheese is a little moldy? It adds to the flavor.) Blueberry jam crepes. The guy knows how to turn any cast-off Auradon grocery shipment into crazy deliciousness. That's the Isle's own brand of magic.

IF YOU THINK THE STORE SMELLS GOOD, YOU SHOULD GET FROLLO'S DAUGHTER, CLAUDINE, TO SHOW YOU THEIR APARTMENT UPSTAIRS. I WENT THERE LAST YEAR TO PICK UP A HAT ONE OF HER FRIENDS NICKED WHEN I WAS TAUNTING TICK-TOCK'S KIN. THE WALLS ARE PAINTED GRAY AND IT'S MISERABLE-LOOKING, BUT I SWEAR THEIR COUCH SMELLS LIKE BANANA CREAM PIE.

Dad's recipe for his
"LARGE AS A BARGE SCRAMBLE"

- Crack five dozen eggs into the largest bowl you can find.

  - Use a bucket if you need to.

- Mix the eggs with a giant fork, or whatever large utensil you can find, until the yellow and white parts are combined.

- Heat up an extra-large pan and melt a stick of butter in it.

  - Pour the eggs into the pan and stir them as they cook, until they are done.

  - Eat them all. Go out into the world.

- BE STRONG.

That's always been my dad's motto: four dozen eggs in the morning to help you get large, five dozen if you want to be big as a barge.

The spinach and egg crepe is the best, but you can usually only get it on Tuesdays, and you have to ask him to triple the eggs. My dad used to take me there when I was a kid, and we'd eat five of them right in a row, one after another. It's how I got so big so fast.

Frollo's no fool, though—he triples the price, too.

• THE MARKETPLACE •

This is your one-stop shop for everything you might need on the Isle. They've got walls and walls of books (if you're into that kind of thing), capes and jackets and top hats. There are torches and candles and tables of food. I found some old fabric there that I used for a dress, and I know most of the staffs on the Isle come from there, too.

HEY, REMEMBER THAT CRACKED CRYSTAL BALL I GOT YOU LAST YEAR FOR YOUR BIRTHDAY? THAT CAME FROM THE MARKETPLACE.

Cool. I have that on a shelf above my bed.

Lady Tremaine's
Curl Up and Dye

Maybe I'd rather not deal with Dizzy, the little twit who worships Evie and Mal, but she works in the best salon on the Isle. Lady Tremaine's CURL UP AND DYE is the only place I'd trust to do my braids, and they always manage to make my highlights the perfect shade of seafoam turquoise. It's the brick building in the center of the city.

DIZZY ⤸

Bad taste in friends, but girl's got style.

You walk in and the walls and floor are spattered with different neon colors, nail polish and hair dyes in every shade possible. There's this cool old car that they use as a counter for the cash register. And there's this picture of Lucifer, Lady Tremaine's cat, hanging on the wall. I would never tell Dizzy (or Lady Tremaine) that I dig the place, but it's actually pretty wicked.

I KNOW IT WELL. I SKIM A LITTLE OFF THE TOP, DAY BY DAY, AND IT ADDS UP. "PASSIVE INCOME" IS THE PHRASE, RIGHT?

LADY TREMAINE'S CURL UP AND DYE

PROS:

- Best braiding on the Isle
- current styles
- wicked dye colors
- young clientele
- cheap prices (when you're as feared as I am, it's FREE.)
- Lady Tremaine never comes downstairs.

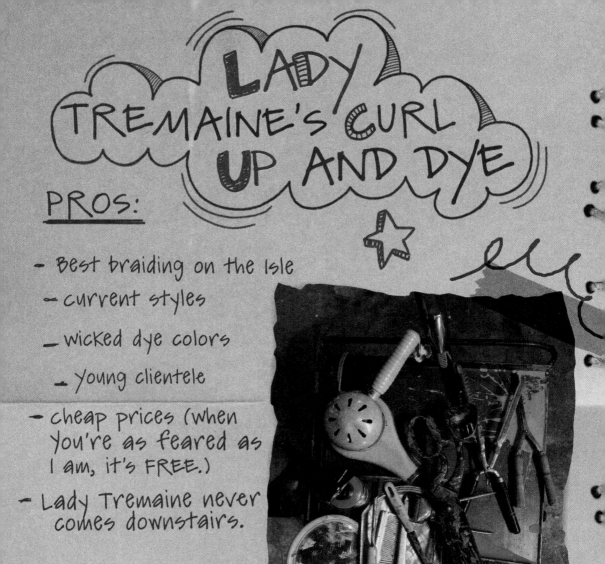

CONS:

- Evie and Mal love it, which means I should hate it.

- Dizzy, Lady Tremaine's granddaughter, still works there.

- The chairs aren't comfy.

- Rinsing your hair in the bathtub is a pain.

As annoying as dealing with Dizzy is, she did style my hair into these braids. I love the blue color she made them.

SHERE KHAN'S PAWNS

This place is so creepy I can't even go inside. The one time I peeked in, it was dark and there were glass cases with snakes in them. who's been there? what's it for?

SNAKES HAVE NEVER BOTHERED ME MUCH, BUT THEN AGAIN I LIKE ANTAGONIZING REPTILES. I WENT THERE WITH MY DAD YEARS AGO WHEN THERE WAS A RAT INFESTATION ON HIS SHIP. THOSE PESKY BUGGERS WERE GETTING INTO EVERYTHING, EATING THROUGH OUR SWEATERS AND SHOES, DEEP-DIVING IN BARRELS OF RICE. SHERE KHAN HAS A WHOLE ARMY OF SNAKES. APPARENTLY, THEY'RE THE SCALY CHILDREN AND GRANDCHILDREN OF KAA.

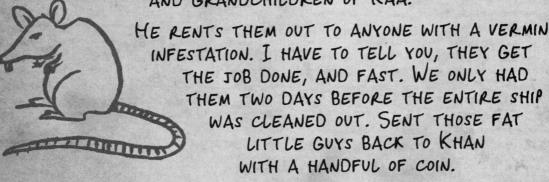

HE RENTS THEM OUT TO ANYONE WITH A VERMIN INFESTATION. I HAVE TO TELL YOU, THEY GET THE JOB DONE, AND FAST. WE ONLY HAD THEM TWO DAYS BEFORE THE ENTIRE SHIP WAS CLEANED OUT. SENT THOSE FAT LITTLE GUYS BACK TO KHAN WITH A HANDFUL OF COIN.

That's . . . disgusting. you didn't care about sleeping on the ship with dozens of snakes?!? I'm getting the heebie-jeebies.

NAH. I WAS ALREADY THIRTEEN— TOO BIG TO BE SWALLOWED.

GASTON'S DUELS WITHOUT RULES

This is my dad's place. I used to work in the stockroom, but then I got in trouble for shooting arrows into the walls. (How was I supposed to know we wouldn't be able to resell them?) Villains come in looking for anything that might be useful during battle: bows and arrows, wooden clubs, axes, pitchforks, swords, and knives. He even has a few massive logs that you can use as a battering ram if you need one. Good for breaking down someone's door.

ARE THE RUMORS TRUE? DO VILLAINS DUEL OUT BACK?

Rumors are always true, Harry.

I don't think I'm supposed to tell anyone, but yes. Villains come from all over the Isle to settle things the old-fashioned way. We have this concrete backyard with a chain-link fence around it. You can't see it from the street. I saw Claude Frollo sword fight with the Horned King. Also saw Mr. Smee and LeFou wrestle each other over a pint of beans.

THEN MAYBE YOU SHOULDN'T BE PUTTING IT IN PRINT. . . .

We're right next to Frollo's Creperie. Come by and check out our new shipment of used cleavers! 30 percent off!

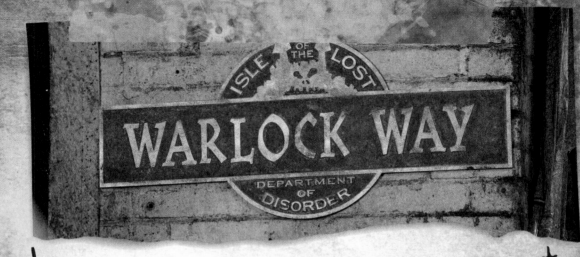

CAULDRON REPAIR

So we've all had to go to this place dozens of times before, but that doesn't make it any less of a hassle. It's at the very darkest, dankest end of Warlock Way. The Horned King started this business when he came to the Isle. He fixes old cauldrons. I heard they were used for magic and mayhem before, but now they're the easiest way to cook two gallons of gruel.

I went there a few weeks ago when my mom's biggest cauldron got a crack in it. It was leaking brine all over the floor. The Horned King did a good job sealing it, but the whole time I was waiting I had to deal with the cauldron-Born trying to scare me. I swear, if I have to stare into any more hollow eye sockets . . .

IT'S LIKE, WE GET IT,
YOU'RE TERRIFYING.
YOU'VE BEEN UNDEAD FOR CENTURIES.
CONGRATULATIONS.

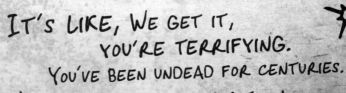

HELL HALL

THIS IS CRUELLA'S PLACE, THE RICKETY OLD VICTORIAN MANSION WITH THE PEELING PAINT AND FALLING-OFF SHUTTERS. IT LOOKED BETTER WHEN SHE HAD THAT TWIT CARLOS TO TAKE CARE OF IT. SHE TREATED HIM LIKE HER OWN PERSONAL CINDERELLA, HAVING HIM MOP AND DUST AND TAKE DOWN THE PEELING WALLPAPER. I REMEMBER BEING IN THERE ONCE AS A KID. A REAL TRASH HEAP. I'D WANTED TO NICK A FEW OF THOSE FUR COATS TO SELL THEM DOWN BY THE WHARF, BUT SHE KEEPS THEM IN A LOCKED CLOSET SURROUNDED BY BEAR TRAPS. DIDN'T WANT TO RISK A LEG JUST TO MAKE SOME COIN. I'VE MET TOO MANY PEG-LEG PIRATES—WHAT A CLICHÉ.

THE CASTLE ACROSS THE WAY

You can't miss this place—it's right down the street from Hell Hall. If Evie wasn't such a stuck-up Auradon kid now, I might feel bad that she was locked in that place for so long. Maleficent banished Evil Queen and Evie to that decrepit castle for a whole decade, just because they didn't invite Mal to Evie's sixth birthday party. In that time, no one saw them—not even on the balconies or through the windows. The only sign that they hadn't died was the vultures that flew in and out every day to deliver supplies. Those ugly birds kept them alive.

I think even _I_ was invited to Evie's sixth birthday party.

URSULA'S FISH & CHIPS SHOPPE

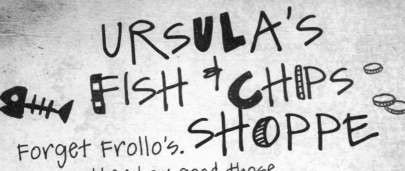

Forget Frollo's.

No matter how good those crepes are, my mom's place is better. we've got the atmosphere and the clientele. we've got smelt fries that melt in your mouth and the only crabby patty on the Isle of the Lost. And we've got waiters with attitude, every villain's favorite side dish.

URSULA'S
FISH & CHIPS

You'll take it how I make it!

2 ANCHOVY
SMOOTHIES . . . . 4 COPPER COINS

1 BOWL CRUSTACEAN
BRAINS . . . . 1 COPPER COIN

TOTAL . . . . **5 COPPER COINS**

Paid for with a handful of glass eyes. The cheapskate didn't leave a tip.

URSULA'S
FISH & CHIPS
You'll take it how I make it!

3 BOWLS OF GRUEL	3 COPPER COINS
2 CRAB SLAB	6 COPPER COINS
1 ORDER SMELT FRIES	3 COPPER COINS
1 CURDLED PUDDING	2 COPPER COINS
1 GLASS OF BRINE	1 COPPER COIN
TOTAL	**15 COPPER COINS**

IOU. —Gil
(Put it on my tab.)

YOU EAT MORE THAN A
SHIP FULL OF PIRATES.

URSULA'S
FISH & CHIPS

You'll take it how I make it!

UNHAPPY HOUR MENU

TEARS OF DESPAIR
(collected from Goblin Wharf)

1 silver coin

SEAWEED SODA
(very limited refills)

1 copper coin

SPOILAGE BREW

1 copper coin

FRIED SHRIMP SHELLS

1 copper coin

SLIGHTLY USED CANDY

1 copper coin for a dozen pieces

ALL BOWLS OF GRUEL — 50% OFF

SO MANY
OPTIONS ...

HOOK'S INLET AND SHACK

TRYING NOT TO BE BITTER ABOUT THIS, BUT I WAS MADE REDUNDANT FROM THIS SHOP YEARS AGO AFTER I GOT CAUGHT SKIMMING COINS FROM THE COFFERS. NEVER MIND, I DIDN'T NEED TO TRUDGE THROUGH THE DAYS THERE ANYWAY. I MUCH PREFER IT OUT ON THE WHARF. BUT IF YOU NEED ANY FISHING SUPPLIES, HOOK'S INLET AND SHACK IS YOUR PLACE.

THEY'VE GOT FISHING RODS AND REELS, LINES, AND TACKLE BOXES. THEY'VE GOT USED WADERS THAT SMELL LIKE GOBLIN FEET AND SOME OF THE MOST UNIQUE LURES YOU'VE EVER SEEN. WHEN I WAS THERE, I WAS IN CHARGE OF FINDING SHINY BITS OF GARBAGE TO THREAD THROUGH THE HOOKS. USED FOIL AND COINS, BROKEN EARRINGS AND OYSTER SHELLS—IT ALL WORKS TO CATCH A BIG ONE.

WHILE YOU'RE THERE, CHECK OUT MY OLD MAN'S BOAT, THE JOLLY ROGER. IT'S USUALLY PARKED RIGHT NEXT TO THE STORE. JUST WATCH YOUR LIMBS, MATEY, 'CAUSE TICK-TOCK'S KIDS ARE SWARMING THE WATER BY THE SHORE.

GOBLIN WHARF

I'm tempted to write about this one just to tell you to stay away from it. It's the only dock on the Isle of the Lost, so all the supplies from Auradon come through there. There are dozens of goblins working to unload all the cargo from the ships that come in. They're wretched, nasty creatures.

Don't talk about them behind their backs, though—they understand human speech, even if they can't carry on a conversation with you. You'll notice there are tons of them hanging around in the center of town now.

Troll Town

I stick out like a sore thumb in Troll Town.
All those trolls trolling around with their
knuckles dragging on the pavement.
They're three feet shorter than me
and they're all so grumpy.

DEVIL HELP YOU IF YOU GET LOST THERE.
ONE WRONG TURN AND YOU'LL BE A KEPT MAN.

Maybe you two don't appreciate Troll Town,
but this is the only place on the Isle you can
get a decent massage. Cruella De Vil and
Anastasia Tremaine are always at Knuckle
Punch. Trolls have huge hands and they love
taking their anger out on someone. Some
people like strikers, but I've heard the
trolls at Knuckle Punch are meaner.

While you're there, check out Claw Trimmers, this nail salon that does cool nail art. Some people think it's wrong that only troll children work there (their hands are smaller) but it's never bothered me. I've been working since I could walk. Besides, a good manicure is a good manicure, right?

SCALLYWAG SWAG

KNUCKLE PUNCH

The Most Brutal Massage in Troll Town

THE TWISTED SISTER

You'll be twisted and turned, cracked and broken.

PRICE: 2 RUBIES

TORTURE & TORMENT

You'll scream out loud from the intensity of this hand massage.

PRICE: 2 SILVER COINS

THE PEOPLE POUNDER

You'll be stomped and jumped on and pounded flat. Trolls will use both feet.

PRICE: 1 GOLD COIN

THE BRUISER

You'll leave black and blue.

PRICE: 1 EMERALD CHIP

ALL CUSTOMERS MUST SIGN LIABILITY WAIVER. KNUCKLE PUNCH IS NOT RESPONSIBLE FOR DISLOCATED SHOULDERS, BROKEN NECKS, OR OTHER SERIOUS INJURIES.

ISLE of the DOOMED!

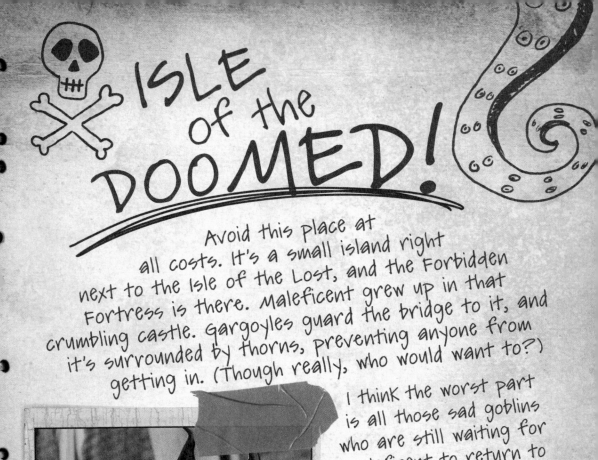

Avoid this place at all costs. It's a small island right next to the Isle of the Lost, and the Forbidden Fortress is there. Maleficent grew up in that crumbling castle. Gargoyles guard the bridge to it, and it's surrounded by thorns, preventing anyone from getting in. (Though really, who would want to?)

I think the worst part is all those sad goblins who are still waiting for Maleficent to return to them. They used to serve her when she lived there, and there are rumors they've been starving on the Isle of the Doomed. Some have even resorted to eating each other. (I heard this from one of the bus goblins in Ma's Kitchen, so take it for what it's worth.)

THE SLOP SHOP

I'm not going to lie, I like this place—even if the goblins who work there are garbage. It's this coffee shop that sells a bunch of discarded Auradon eats, like moldy buns, stale muffins, and rotten eggs. The coffee is stronger than Gil. One tip, though: eat your meal slowly. Like, we're talking one bite every ten minutes. Because as soon as you're done, the goblins will clear your dishes and try to rush you out.

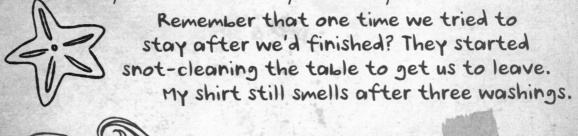

Remember that one time we tried to stay after we'd finished? They started snot-cleaning the table to get us to leave. My shirt still smells after three washings.

I've been there every week for my entire life, and I still have no idea what this menu says. I just look at the food in the case and point to what I want.

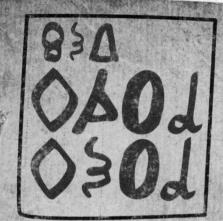

ⵣⵉⴰ ⴱⵯⴷⵙⵇⴱⴷⵡ ⵇⵙⵇⴱⴷⵙ

ⵅⵇⵢⴷⴷ ⵙⴷ ⴱⵯⴷⵙⵇⴱⴷⵡ ⵉⵅⵯ ⴱⵣⴷⴷⵯ,
ⵏⴷⵙⴻⵢⴷⵡ ⵉⵅⵯ ⵙⴷⵇⵢⴷⵖ
ⴷⵏⵙⴻⴷ: ‖ ⴷⵏⴻⴷⵙⴷⴷ

← THESE ARE MY FAVORITE! THIRD-DAY DONUTS! SO GOOD . . .

ⴱⵇⴷⴱⵉⴷⴷ ⵉⵅⵯ ⴱⵇⴷⴷⵯⴷⵡ

ⵅⵇⵢⴷⴷ ⵇⴻⴷⴷⵡ ⵇⵉⴷ ⵢⵇⵉⵯ ⴼⵣⴷⴱ ⵣⵉⴷ
ⴷⵯⴱⵇⵇⴻⵡ ⵉⵅⵯ ⵇⵣⵙⵇ ⵉⵉⵅⵯ ⴷⴱⵇⵇⴱⴷⴷ
ⴷⵏⵙⴻⴷ: ‖ ⵇⵣⴷⵙⴷⴷⵙ ⴻⵇⵙⴷⵇ

ⵣⵉⴰ ⴷⵇⵇⴷⵏⴷ ⴷⵇⵣⵉⴱⴷⴷ

ⵅⵇⵢⴷⴷ ⵙⴷ ⵇⴱⵇⴱⵇⴱⵯ ⵉⵢ
ⴷⵏⵙⴻⴷ: ‖ ⵢⵇⵉⵯ ⴻⵇⵙⴷ

NO WAY you know what that says.

YEAH, NO. KIDDING. I'VE GOT NO CLUE.

REMEMBER WHEN THAT REALLY HAIRY GOBLIN, MOE, SLIPPED THIS LOVE LETTER UNDER YOUR PLATE, UMA? THE LOOK ON YOUR FACE: WORTH MORE THAN A TREASURE CHEST FULL OF GOLD.

Again, you have no idea what it says. Maybe he was just . . . asking me about the donuts.

UM . . .

he definitely has a crush on you.

HOW TO DEAL WITH GOBLINS

These creatures are the nastiest of the nasty— and I don't mean that as a compliment. Since King Ben put a lot of them out of work, they've gotten meaner than they ever were before. If you run into any, make sure you:

1) Don't speak to them unless you absolutely have to.

2) Don't look them directly in the eye.

3) Don't get too close. (They've been known to lunge and hit or grab people when they're angry.)

4) Don't say anything around them you wouldn't want everyone on the Isle to know. They're notorious gossips.

#WICKEDLY COOL

THE FUTURE IS
BLEAK

The nastiest clairvoyants you'll ever meet work at Frollo's Fortune Teller. Can they actually predict your future? Maybe. Can they tap into your deepest fears, come up with the cruelest personal nightmares, and have them come true? One hundred percent.

You can know every place on the Isle of the Lost, every alley and dead end. You can learn about the backyard duels at Gaston's or find the trapdoor in the storage room of Frollo's creperie, the one that leads to the Isle sewer system (perfect for quick getaways). And you can know each goblin by name and how to trick them into being nice to you. But you won't get anywhere without the right attitude. And by "right attitude," I mean the ability to dominate everyone you meet.

Ever since Mal, that traitorous Goody Two-shoes, called me shrimpy when I was a kid, I knew I had to be number one on the Isle. Anything less means taunting and teasing and buckets of shrimp guts on your head. surviving is not enough. From that day on, I've been obsessed with . . .

RULING

MORE VILLAIN THAN MAL

THE ISLE

SCHOOLS 2 RULE

DRAGON HALL

This is where the Isle's youngest villains go to get a head start on wickedness, though they have an upper-level school now, too. It's in an old tomb. (Don't worry, they cleared the bodies out, though it would've been cooler if they hadn't.) Dr. Facilier founded it ages ago, and there's a rumor he has an office somewhere inside, even though it's impossible to find. We did some time there, learning from the mistakes of the villains that came before us, before going to Serpent Prep. Dr. Facilier thinks it's important to be prepared for when the barrier finally falls.

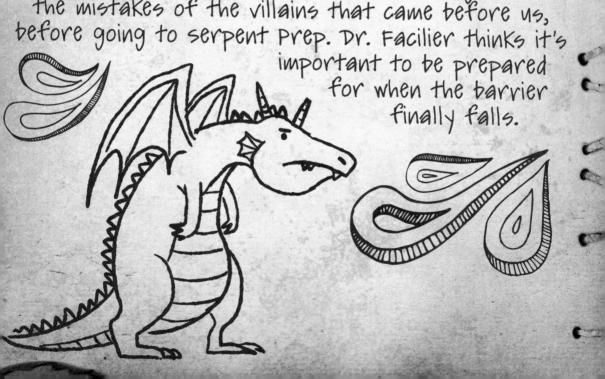

I still have nightmares about the Athenaeum of Evil. It's this library that only Dr. Facilier has the key to. I must've walked by it a hundred times. There's a spider the size of a cauldron outside the door. It has these huge hairy legs and pincers that could break your arm.

I HAVE A LOT OF GOOD MEMORIES OF THE CEMETERY OUTSIDE. KICKING OVER HEADSTONES AND STOMPING ON GRAVES . . .

WITCH SCHOOL

Never been in this place, would never want to. It's a crumbling building in the middle of downtown. The windows are covered in soot and there are always strange flashes of light and explosions coming from the basement. I heard Mad Maddy is a student there. . . .

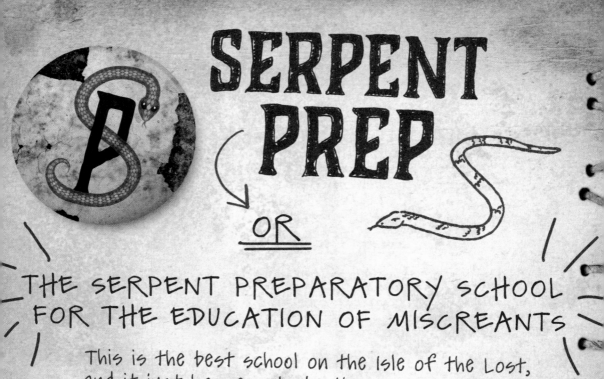

SERPENT PREP

OR

THE SERPENT PREPARATORY SCHOOL FOR THE EDUCATION OF MISCREANTS

This is the best school on the Isle of the Lost, and it just happens to be the one we go to. The place is not far from Gaston's house, on the opposite side of the Isle from Dragon Hall. Just look for the main gate—there are two giant stone serpent statues guarding the entrance.

Since it's right on the water, the whole place is covered with moss and sea slime. It's damp and dark and the stone walls are sweaty to the touch. There are torches lining every hallway and there's a high tower with a long, winding staircase. From the top classrooms you can see the entire Isle, coast to coast.

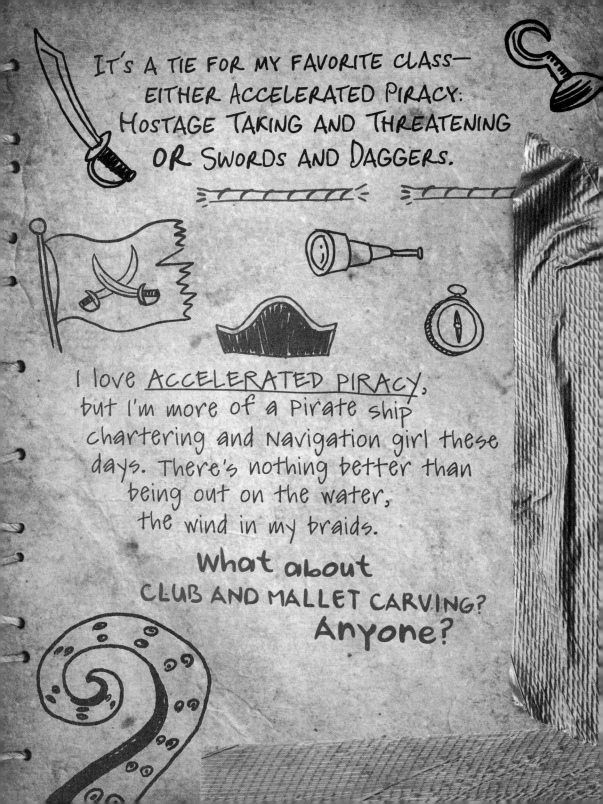

IT'S A TIE FOR MY FAVORITE CLASS—
EITHER ACCELERATED PIRACY:
HOSTAGE TAKING AND THREATENING
OR SWORDS AND DAGGERS.

I love <u>ACCELERATED PIRACY</u>,
but I'm more of a pirate ship
chartering and navigation girl these
days. There's nothing better than
being out on the water,
the wind in my braids.

What about
CLUB AND MALLET CARVING?
Anyone?

LOOK! I FOUND ONE OF MY OLD DRAGON HALL REPORT CARDS IN MY DAD'S TREASURE CHEST. I THINK THIS WAS THE PROUDEST HE'S EVER BEEN OF ME.

You killed it!

I hated this class. Mother Gothel jabbering on about villain photography. Who cares? What does it matter if you can take a good selfie or not? I never needed to show anyone my phone to show them how fierce I was.

And isn't it unfair that Evie got an A?!? She's been staring at that magic mirror since she was a baby.

HARRY HOOK

DRAGON HALL

REPORT CARD

SELFISHNESS 101 · · · · · · · · · · · B

EVIL SCHEMES AND NASTY PLOTS · · · · A

P.E. · · · · · · · · · · · · · · · · · F

WICKEDNESS · · · · · · · · · · · · · B+

WEIRD SCIENCE · · · · · · · · · · · · F

VILLAINY THROUGH THE AGES · · · · · C

SEMESTER AVERAGE · · · · · **C**

This was always my favorite class. I could listen to stories about my dad for hours.

DRAGON HALL TWERPS

There's nothing better than sneaking onto Dragon Hall property and playing tricks on those DH twerps. I once had my whole pirate crew lie in wait behind the tombstones in the cemetery. We dressed in our darkest clothes and put ghost makeup on our faces. When the Dragon Hall first graders came out, we jumped up and pretended we were undead. Those little twits scattered like rats.

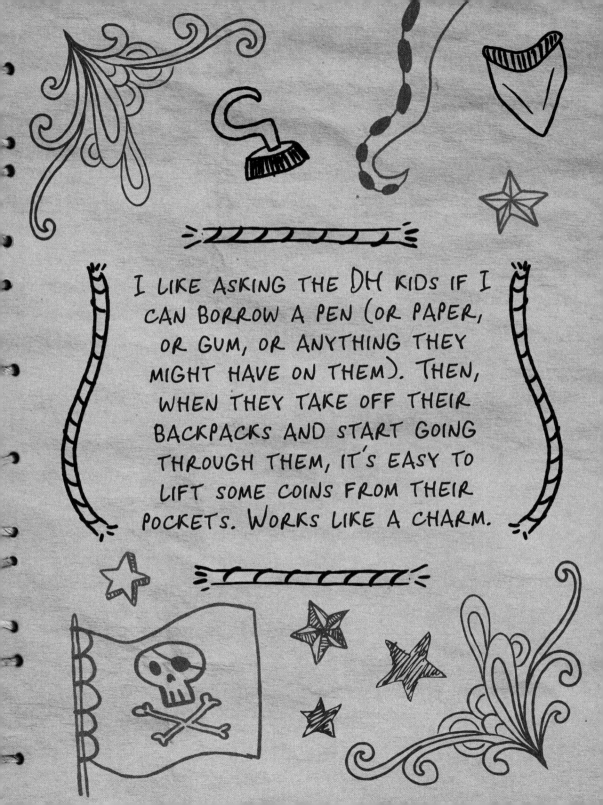

I LIKE ASKING THE DH KIDS IF I CAN BORROW A PEN (OR PAPER, OR GUM, OR ANYTHING THEY MIGHT HAVE ON THEM). THEN, WHEN THEY TAKE OFF THEIR BACKPACKS AND START GOING THROUGH THEM, IT'S EASY TO LIFT SOME COINS FROM THEIR POCKETS. WORKS LIKE A CHARM.

DRAGON HALL
SUPERL

MOST LIKELY TO
~~SUCCEED AT ALL COSTS~~
BETRAY THE ISLE
MAL

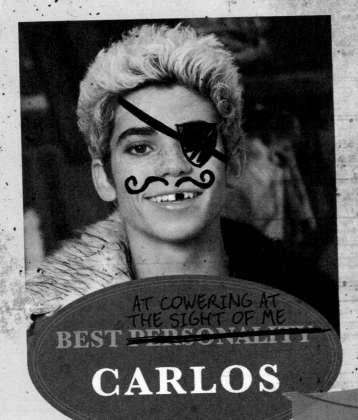

L**ATIVES**

AT COWERING AT
THE SIGHT OF ME

BEST ~~PERSONALITY~~

CARLOS

MOST FASHIONABLE

LIKELY TO FOLLOW MAL

EVIE AROUND LIKE A PUPPY

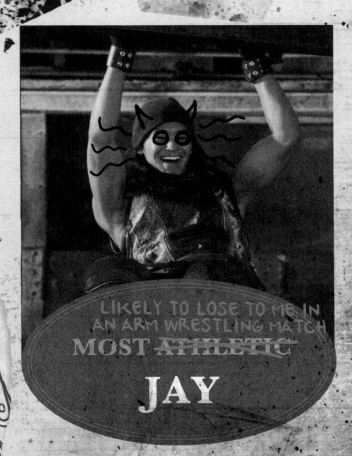

LIKELY TO LOSE TO ME IN
AN ARM WRESTLING MATCH
MOST ~~ATHLETIC~~

JAY

SERPENT PREP

BORE-A-DON VS.
~~AURADON~~ PREP

SERPENT PREP

PROS
- No fakes or phonies
- Rules are meant to be broken
- You don't have to pretend to be someone you're not
  - Grades don't matter
  - Some of the evilest villains teach there
  - Best clubs and activities on the Isle

CONS
- No one takes school seriously
  - Can't hear over all the yelling and fights breaking out
  - Hopelessness
  - Constantly getting sick because the dungeons are so damp

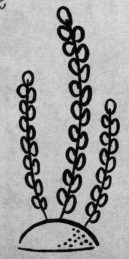

AURADON PREP

PROS

- Fresh food
- sunlight and a grassy quad
- students want to succeed
- Not being on the Isle
- Huge dorm rooms
- Magic is allowed in Auradon
- weekend trips anywhere you want

I never even knew what grass was before I saw pictures of Auradon Prep

CONS

- Under King Ben's rule
- Easy to get expelled
- Mal and Evie are there
- Everyone's fake nice; wouldn't know who to trust
- A million rules
- who cares about cheerleading and tourney?!

REIGN OF THE SEA

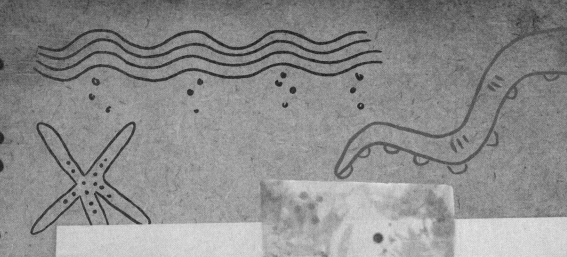

SERPENT PREP
SCHEDULE FOR SPRING SEMESTER

UMA, DAUGHTER OF URSULA

FIRST PERIOD	ACCELERATED PIRACY
SECOND PERIOD	UNDERSTANDING GOBLIN SPEECH
THIRD PERIOD	CHARTERING AND NAVIGATION
FOURTH PERIOD	LUNCH
FIFTH PERIOD	COIN AND JEWEL CALCULUS
SIXTH PERIOD	ADVANCED WICKEDNESS
SEVENTH PERIOD	UNDER THE SEA: SCIENCE BELOW THE SURFACE
EIGHTH PERIOD	HISTORY OF THE ISLE

A VK HAPPILY EVER AFTER

~~rince Ben and Lady Mal~~
~~tinue to enjoy their time~~

IF THE ISLE'S TAUGHT ME ANYTHING, IT'S THAT THERE ARE NO HAPPILY-EVER-AFTERS

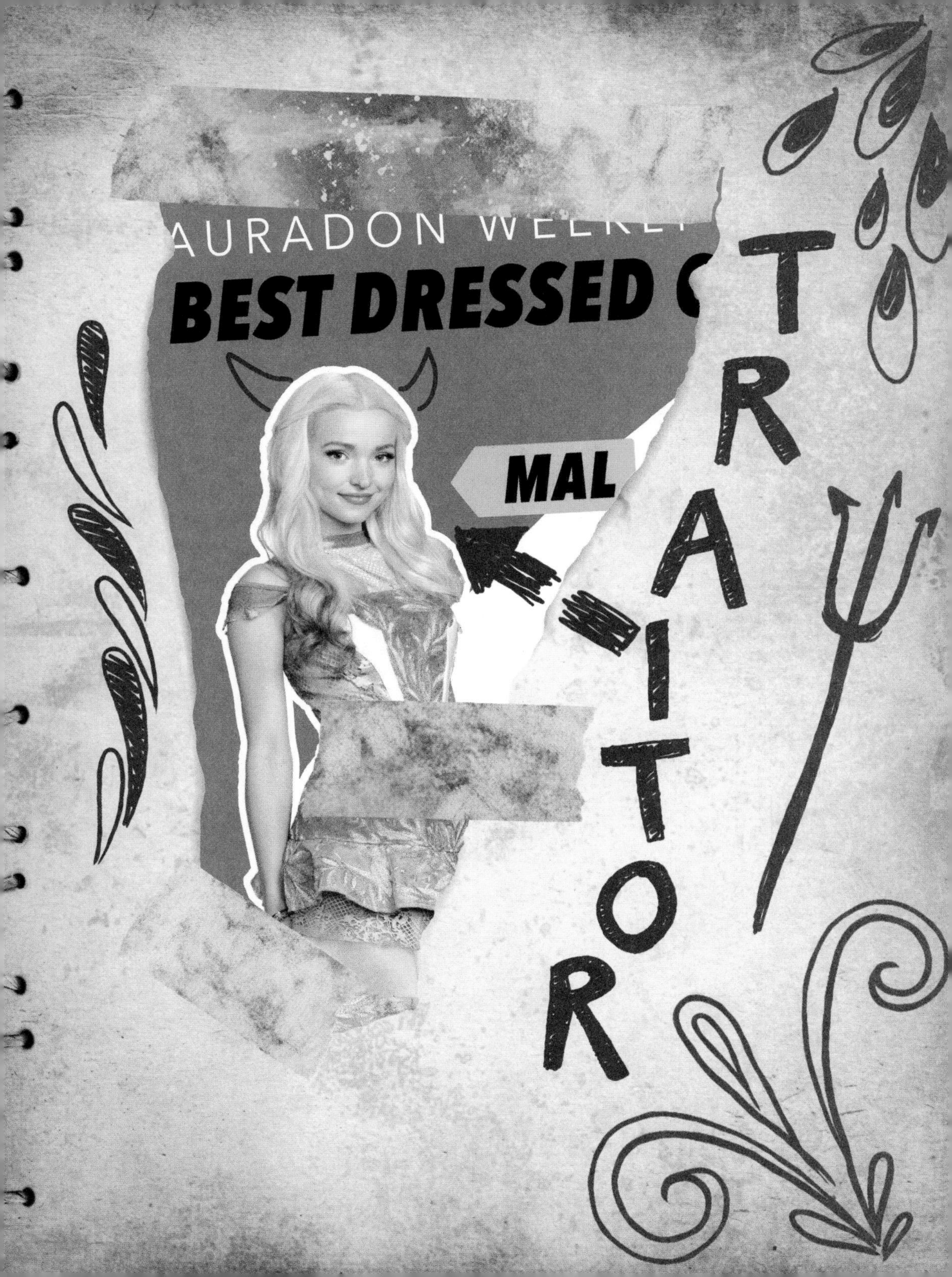
AURADON
BEST DRESSED
MAL
TRAITOR

EVIL EXTRACURRICULARS

The best thing about Serpent Prep is that our clubs are cooler than the wharf winds. Anything you can imagine, we have. It's one of the reasons Serpent Prep kids are tougher, cleverer, and stronger than any other kids on the Isle. Who needs coin calculus when you know how to wrestle a crocodile into submission?

CROC WRESTLING

I ADMIT, IT'S AN IMPRESSIVE SKILL TO HAVE. TOOK ME SIX YEARS OF BEING IN THE CROC WRESTLING CLUB TO PERFECT MY CROC TAKEDOWN. WE MEET EVERY WEDNESDAY AFTERNOON DOWN AT HOOK'S INLET. THE SHALLOWS THERE ARE SWARMING WITH TICK-TOCK'S CHILDREN AND GRANDCHILDREN. THEY HAD US START SMALL, TRAINING WITH SOME OF THE YOUNGER CROCS, BUT NOW I'M WRESTLING THE EIGHT-FOOT ONES. YOU HAVEN'T LIVED UNTIL YOU'VE ESCAPED A CROC'S JAWS.

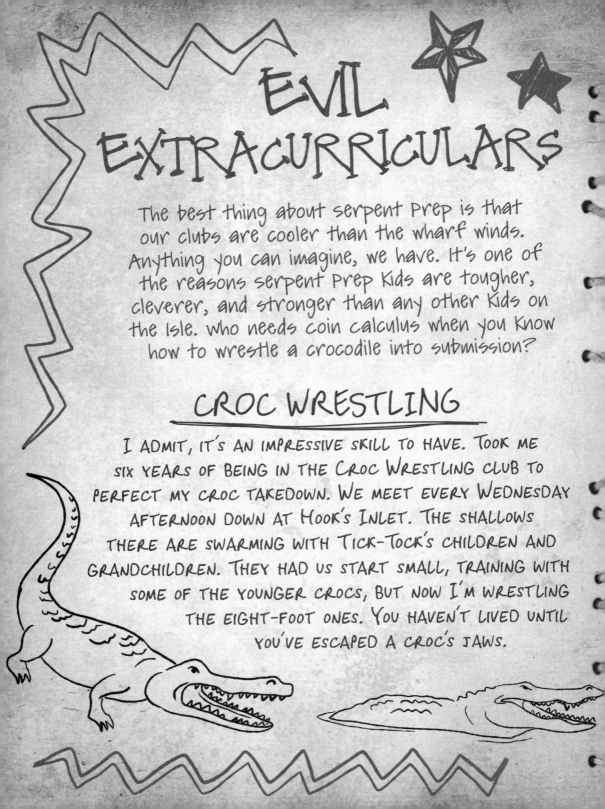

COMPETITIVE LIFTING

Tables, chairs, people sitting in chairs, treasure chests, cauldrons, even a rotted wooden dresser full of clothes—there's nothing you can't lift after a few months in the Competitive Lifting club. I've been captain for three years now. My most memorable lifts were a bench with three Serpent Prep girls sitting on it, two scooters (one in each hand), and a barrel full of goblins.

That was one of the reasons I let you in my crew. There must've been ten of them shoved in there, probably more.

SHARK
SWIM TEAM

when this club started, some serpent
Prep Kids were all "we can't swim with
sharks—the sharks are going to bite us!
I don't want to lose my leg for some stupid club!"
But I Knew better. The sea has always been my
second home. I've been swimming in the water
around the Isle since before I could walk.

I was one of the first students to sign up for
shark swim Team, and I've been team captain
ever since. Those practices have helped me out
more than a few times, like when our rowboat
Seriously, Uma—   got stuck in a massive storm and
thanks.   I had to save gil from drowning.
      Living on an island, you have to be a good
swimmer, and swimming with sharks makes you
one of the best. Besides, it's not dangerous
if you're smart about it. I give my team some
warnings before every practice or meet.

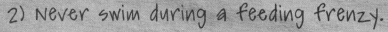

1) Never swim with chum in the water.

2) Never swim during a feeding frenzy.

3) Never swim by a pirate ship. (Sharks are used to eating hostages there.)

4) when swimming with a shark, grip the fin tightly and keep your head above water. Keep your legs on either side of its back.

5) If your shark starts to circle you like it's going to attack, swim below it and punch it hard in the stomach. It just needs a reminder who's boss.

Hey! You do the same thing to me sometimes.

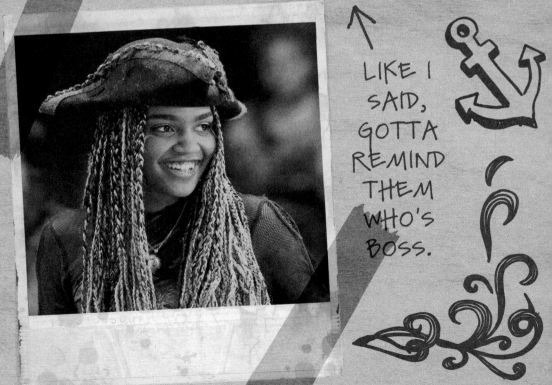

LIKE I SAID, GOTTA REMIND THEM WHO'S BOSS.

WICKED BEAUTIES

Ugh. I don't even know where to begin with this one. Drizella Tremaine runs this club at Serpent Prep, and it's basically a bunch of girls learning how to be mean and betray their friends. I get it, Shark Swim Team isn't for everyone, but getting life lessons from Drizella Tremaine once a week?
NO, THANK YOU.

SPEAKING WITH TROLLS

THIS ONE'S FOR THE MORE STUDIOUS SERPENT PREP KIDS. THEY INVITE A TROLL IN EVERY THURSDAY AFTER SCHOOL AND HAVE LONG (BOOOOOOORING) DISCUSSIONS WITH IT, GOING ON ABOUT EVERYTHING TROLL LIFE AND TROLL LIVING. WHAT'S IT LIKE TO EAT SLUGS AND BEETLES FOR DINNER? DON'T THEIR FEET GET COLD, WALKING BAREFOOT EVERYWHERE? THAT KIND OF THING.

Translation: this club
is for lame-os.

RAT TRAPPING

Clay Clayton is the faculty advisor for the club. I'd wanted Dad to do it, but he's too busy running his shop these days, and his new wife is pretty demanding. (She takes up all his time.) We go around the Isle with nets and traps and catch all the vermin we can. I've even caught some snakes and ravens. Clay takes the traps out to the other side of the Isle after we're done and lets them all go, or that's what he says. The goblins say he has a deal with Brews & Stews and gets a copper coin for every rat he gives them. I don't know if that's true, but I never eat there, just to be safe. . . .

IT'S DEFINITELY TRUE. WHY DO YOU THINK ALL THE MEAT THERE IS SO SMALL?

with tiny bones, and legs . . . yuck.

SCAMMERS AND PICKPOCKETS

I'M THE FOUNDER AND PRESIDENT OF THIS CLUB. WE'VE RUN EVERY GREAT SCAM THE ISLE HAS EVER SEEN. THE BEST WAS A FEW YEARS BACK, WHEN WE WALKED AROUND PRETENDING WE'D FOUND A BAG OF JEWELS IN A WHARF CAVE. WE TALKED LOUDLY ABOUT IT IN THE TOWN SQUARE, RIGHT BY THE MARKET, AND THEN LURED A FEW TWITS INTO AN ALLEYWAY. WE NICKED EVERYTHING THEY HAD, RIGHT DOWN TO THEIR SKIVVIES.

THEY DESERVED IT FOR TRYING TO RIP US OFF.

SEA PONIES!!

I never did get to have a sea pony of my very own, but being in this club has helped take away the sting. These adorable, sweet little creatures are the cutest things in the ocean. They're also rare around the Isle and almost impossible to catch. Serpent Prep has two resident sea ponies, Cornelius and Greta, and the students in the club rotate taking care of them. I've taken them home twice since joining, and I'll never get tired of watching them swim around their tank. I swear Greta recognizes me, too. She always comes right up to the glass and stares at me with those sweet little eyes, and I get real close and—

ERRR, I better stop talking about sea ponies. People are going to think I've gone soft.

THEY'RE YOUR GREATEST WEAKNESS.

SEA PONIES

SCALLYWAG SWAG

we may not have a lot on the Isle of the Lost, but we never let that show. Buttons, broken earrings, seashells, and fishing nets; chains and rope and leather that's cracked and worn—you can find materials in the wharf, in the trash, or in the Isle's pawn shops. You just need some vision and some skills to pull it all together.

I've always taken pride in my Isle style. wharf rats will compliment me on my boots or all the tiny details on my tricorn hat. I have to admit it feels good to walk down the dock Knowing I look good—it feels <u>real</u> good. Leading a whole crew of ruffians isn't easy, and my style commands respect. If you want to be a pirate queen, you've got to dress like one. . . .

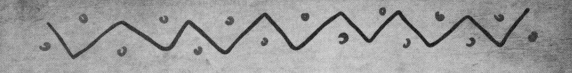

1) Learn how to sew. If you manage to find someone selling a cool outfit, it's going to be ten times as much coin as it should be. Make your own jackets, skirts, and tank tops (and everything you can, really).

2) Learn how to scavenge. There are cool materials all over the Isle; you just need to have an eye for them. I like to use the insides of oyster shells to add some glam to my outfits. Find what works for you.

3) Only buy what you need, but know what you need to buy. Belt buckles and hats are hard to come by, so you'll have to get them at the market. Boots, gloves, and bags are tricky, too (though you'll still have to accessorize them). You should be able to scavenge and make everything else.

4) Know the shortcuts. Fishhooks work for jewelry (especially earrings). Layered netting is great for skirts. Old couches and chairs can be taken apart—use that fabric for jackets and vests.

5) Protect what you've got. A full wardrobe is more valuable than gold. Make sure you keep it locked up in a place no one else knows about except you. For a while, I kept mine in a barrel behind my mom's shop.

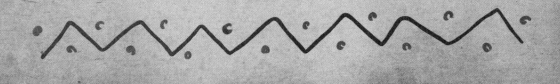

PIRATE SWAG

My Isle style

seriously, don't feel bad if you can't pull an outfit like this together right away. I've been building my wardrobe for years, collecting tiny bits of fabric and shells, finding the perfect pieces in the market. If you go to the bazaar right before it closes, you'll get the best deals. Hawkers can haggle is all I'm going to say.

Broken oyster shells for glitter and shine

PAINTED COTTON: it's one of the easiest materials to find on the Isle, as long as you don't mind holes.

I made this jacket out of a broken armchair that came in from Auradon. I ripped apart the leather and reassembled it.

Old burlap sacks from the wharf that I cut into strips and spray-painted to make them stiff

Anyone who's anyone wears fingerless gloves.

old fishing nets

Decorated with broken jewelry found at Jafar's Junk shop. Old necklaces and charm bracelets are the best.

PIRATE
STYLE
RULE Z

ISLE

ORIGINATOR

ATTITUDE
is Everything

I came up with this on a slow day at Ma's shop. I was scribbling on the back of an old receipt, just messing around, when I realized it was actually looking like something pretty cool. Now I think of it as the unofficial symbol of Uma, daughter of Ursula—pirate queen.

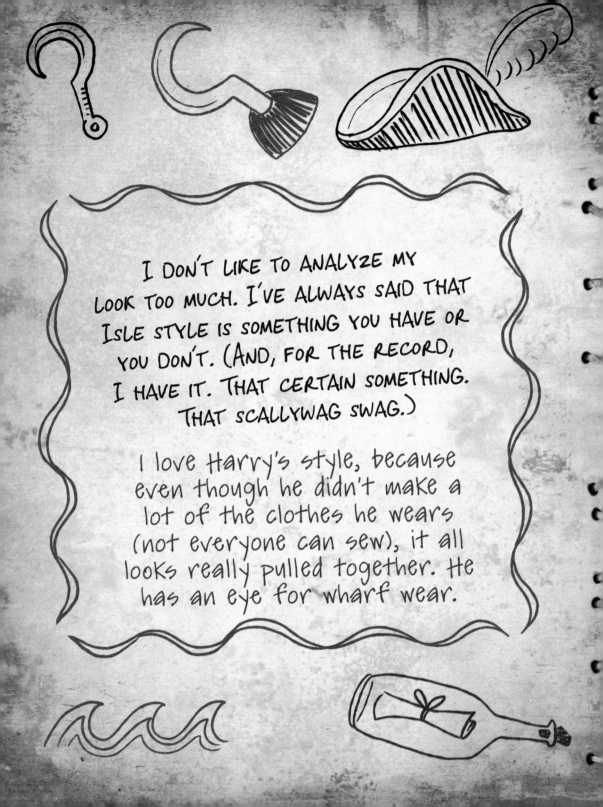

I DON'T LIKE TO ANALYZE MY LOOK TOO MUCH. I'VE ALWAYS SAID THAT ISLE STYLE IS SOMETHING YOU HAVE OR YOU DON'T. (AND, FOR THE RECORD, I HAVE IT. THAT CERTAIN SOMETHING. THAT SCALLYWAG SWAG.)

I love Harry's style, because even though he didn't make a lot of the clothes he wears (not everyone can sew), it all looks really pulled together. He has an eye for wharf wear.

I'M TRASH AT SEWING, SO MY DAD GAVE ME THIS JACKET FROM WHEN HE WAS A WEE PIRATE LAD. IT'S RIPPED AND DIRTY, JUST THE WAY I LIKE IT. MY FAVORITE PART IS THE LABEL—HE WROTE HOOK ON IT IN SQUID INK.

I LIKE THE HOLES IN MY SHIRT. THEY LET THE WHARF WINDS IN.

YOU CAN'T HAVE ENOUGH PLACES TO HANG YOUR FISHING NETS, CHAINS, OR ROPES. I CLIPPED ON THESE EXTRA HOOKS AND LOOPS MYSELF.

BEST ACCESSORY FOR A PIRATE. NOTHING SAYS "I'LL GIVE YOU A SECOND SMILE" LIKE A RAZOR-SHARP HOOK.

BOOTS I NICKED FROM SOME TWIT DOZING UNDER THE DOCKS

Remember that time you accidentally stole MY boots? I took them off to go swimming and came back and they were gone. Then, the next day, I saw Harry wearing them.

Not at all surprising.

My mom taught me how to sew when I was a kid, and I've made a bunch of my clothes since then. Gaston Jr. and Gaston III always try to get me to make them jackets or vests and stuff, so I've somehow gotten suckered into being the family designer. (Those ripped tank tops they wear are all me.) Being crafty on the Isle gives you more than a leg up. Just 'cause we're bad doesn't mean we have to look bad, too.

Grow your hair long for a rugged look.

I found this charm at a stall in the market. It's a good reminder of Beast and everything he did to my family.

I paint my gloves gold to make them more unique.

I'd rather wear jeans than anything else. It's good for working down at the wharf. (You don't have to be as careful as you do with leather pants.) I like to cover the holes with scraps of fabric I've found.

I know Uma said you have to buy belts at the market, but here's a secret... You can find broken and cracked ones in the trash bin outside the fish and chips shoppe. They rush to buy most of the belts that come from Auradon in bulk without looking at them first, then toss the ones they can't sell.

VILLAINS FROM

THE DEEP

HATS ~~OFF~~ ON

They say only confident people wear hats, and I'm living proof of that. Accessorize your pirate outfit with a three-point hat or a tied kerchief. Stick an old seagull feather in it to add some Isle flair.

People like to use seagull feathers in their hats 'cause they're everywhere, but I found this raven feather on the other side of the Isle. It gives the look more of an edge.

Technically this is called a tricorn, but who would actually use that word in public? Not me. I just call it my pirate hat, because it completes my pirate look.

Part of a fishing net adds layers.

Found seashells and starfish, spray-painted to pop.

Leather scraps I found in the trash bin outside Gaston's Duels without Rules.

I like my kerchief 'cause it's easy.
Keeps my hair out of my eyes during
sword fights and lifting competitions. I don't know,
I don't really make a big deal out of how I tie it.
Just a knot in the back somewhere.

I found this fabric scrap in a shipment from Auradon.
There's a rumor it came from one of Beast's dress
shirts, which makes me like it even more. I sewed
some leather on the edges to make it stronger.

IT DOESN'T HAVE TO BE AN EITHER/OR THING. YOU CAN WEAR A
KERCHIEF AND A HAT. THAT'S WHAT I DO. I SWITCH OUT THE
KERCHIEFS ALL THE TIME AND USE DIFFERENT COLORS, BECAUSE THEY
GET SOAKED WITH SWEAT WHEN I'M WORKING DOWN BY THE WHARF.

FORGET RAVEN
FEATHERS—
THIS IS A
SEAGULL'S
FEATHER. STILL
SMELLS LIKE
THE OCEAN.

BRAIDED ROPE
I GLUED ON

SOME CHARMS
THAT WASHED
IN FROM A
SHIPWRECK

FIND A LONG SCRAP OF FABRIC SO IT
CAN HANG DOWN FROM UNDER THE HAT.
TIE IT ANY WAY YOU WANT.

Harry spent hours piecing my mom's broken necklace back together for me. It shattered into a dozen pieces when she battled Eric and his ship. We used this sticky gruel as glue, but when it was all together, we were still missing one tiny gold sliver. I found it in the locket my mom gave me, and voila! It was perfect and whole again.

Back when villains were able to use magic, this shell held the souls of hundreds of sea creatures. My mom even trapped Ariel's voice inside it. It'll never have its full power on the Isle of the Lost, but it's connected to King Triton's trident, and we used the shell like a compass to find the trident at the bottom of the sea. Too bad that traitor Mal got to it first. . . .

A LOOK THAT COULD KILL

I STARTED USING SOOT AROUND MY EYES A WHILE BACK. YOU SEE, IT GIVES ME A MORE INTIMIDATING STARE. AND ON THE ISLE OF THE LOST, ANY EDGE YOU CAN GET SHOULD BE USED AND EXPLOITED. IF YOU WANT TO GET THIS LOOK, YOU CAN USE SOME SOOT AND A PAINTBRUSH OR, EVEN BETTER, SOME USED MAKEUP PENCILS FROM AURADON. (THOSE COST SOME COIN.)

1. LINE YOUR EYES ALL THE WAY AROUND.

2. MAKE THE LINE A LITTLE LONGER AT THE OUTSIDE CORNERS.

3. SMUDGE IT ALL TO GET THAT SMOLDERING LOOK.

4. GO OUT AND TERRIFY PEOPLE.

UP TO NO GOOD

WAYS TO BE WICKED

I can't watch the Auradon News Network without laughing. All those Goody Two-shoes, with their noses stuck high in the air, going on about balls and feasts and how much they love to summer in Camelot Heights. Pictures of Belle's tea parties and Fairy Godmother giving lectures about charitable contributions.

PUH-LEEEEEASE.

Maybe the Isle is drab, and maybe we're stuck behind the barrier, but we sure do make the most of it. Every day I wake up, throw the curtains open to look at the clouds and smog, and choose <u>bad</u>. Before I even step outside, I'm thinking of all the ways to be wicked and rotten to the core. . . .

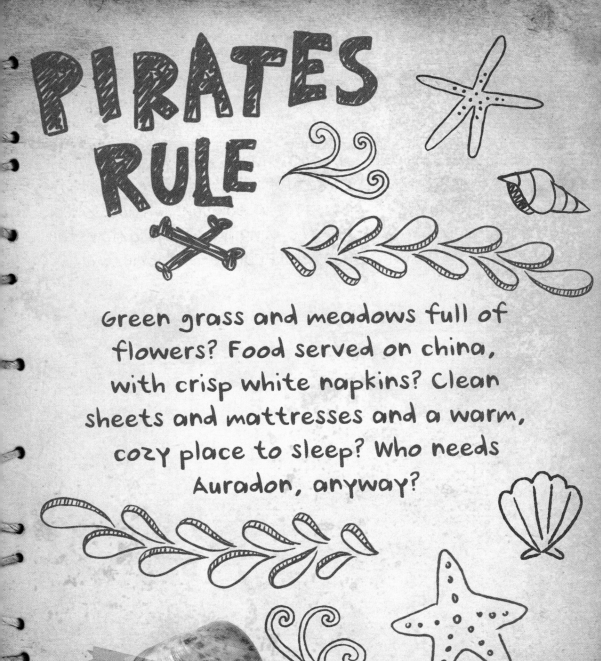

PIRATES RULE

Green grass and meadows full of flowers? Food served on china, with crisp white napkins? Clean sheets and mattresses and a warm, cozy place to sleep? Who needs Auradon, anyway?

There's nothing better than a perfectly planned food fight. Maybe your enemies are sitting across the slop shop, giving you the stink eye. They're ready to brawl in the alley out back, but you have other plans. . . .

We've been in hundreds of food fights and we know what to throw and what to duck. Not all foods are created equal when it comes to exploding in someone's face. Check out these tips for when you're slinging sludge out in the wild—from Ma's shop to Frollo's creperie.

SNAKE EGGS

Small and filled with the nastiest juice you can imagine. They're perfect because they'll explode all over someone like a water balloon. You can't get the stink out of your clothes.

CRAB SANDWICH

Don't even bother. sandwiches fly apart in the air. The bun will go one way while the patty usually falls on the floor. They are not aerodynamic.

CURDLED CREAM

IF YOU THROW IT IN THE CARTON, IT'LL EXPLODE AND LEAVE WHITE CLUMPS EVERYWHERE.

ROTTEN APPLES

DUCK THESE. DO NOT LET THEM HIT YOU. Even though they're rotten, they're hard as rocks. I've gotten two black eyes from these.

SLUG SLIME

I'll throw a whole fistful of this. It's heavy and stays together in the air.

EEL TAILS

Remember that time I hit Mad Maddy with one, and it landed right in her mouth?

SHE SCREAMED FOR HOURS.

GRUEL

There's nothing better. I once dumped a whole cauldron on Jace, Jasper's son.

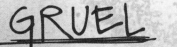

STALE MUFFINS

I LIKE THESE BECAUSE THEY'RE HARD, BUT NOT TOO HARD. THEY FEEL LIKE FAIR GAME.

I try not to throw them if they're more than a week old. Slop shop muffins, yes. The ones from Miserable Morning?

No way.

RASPBERRY JAM CREPE

Don't throw these. Ever. They don't do anything, and they're also too delicious to waste. If a fight breaks out in Frollo's, try to hide your plate under the table and throw someone else's order.

SEAWEED SMOOTHIE

If you didn't serve them in those huge glasses these would be easier to throw.

Is that a complaint?

No, no. Of course not.

MOLDY JELLY DONUTS

These are cool because if you throw them hard enough, the jelly squirts out the side. I've seen it shoot four or five feet.

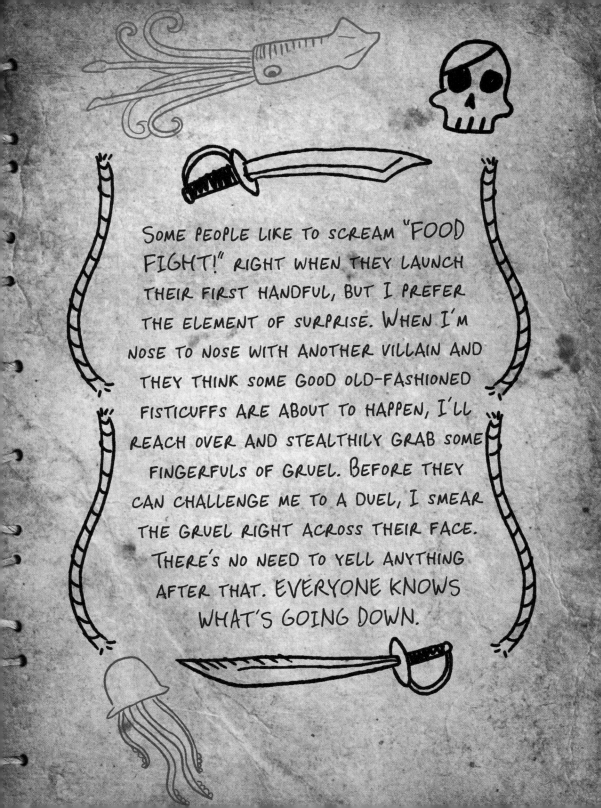

Some people like to scream "FOOD FIGHT!" right when they launch their first handful, but I prefer the element of surprise. When I'm nose to nose with another villain and they think some good old-fashioned fisticuffs are about to happen, I'll reach over and stealthily grab some fingerfuls of gruel. Before they can challenge me to a duel, I smear the gruel right across their face. There's no need to yell anything after that. EVERYONE KNOWS WHAT'S GOING DOWN.

MARKING ~~YOUR~~ TERRITORY

Living on the Isle of the Lost means staking out a place to call your own. For me, it's always been the area of the wharf around Ma's fish and chips shop. My pirates and I own those streets. My ship, the <u>Lost Revenge</u>, was parked there for ages. That's why you'll see our skulls everywhere—they tell everyone that they're on <u>MY</u> turf.

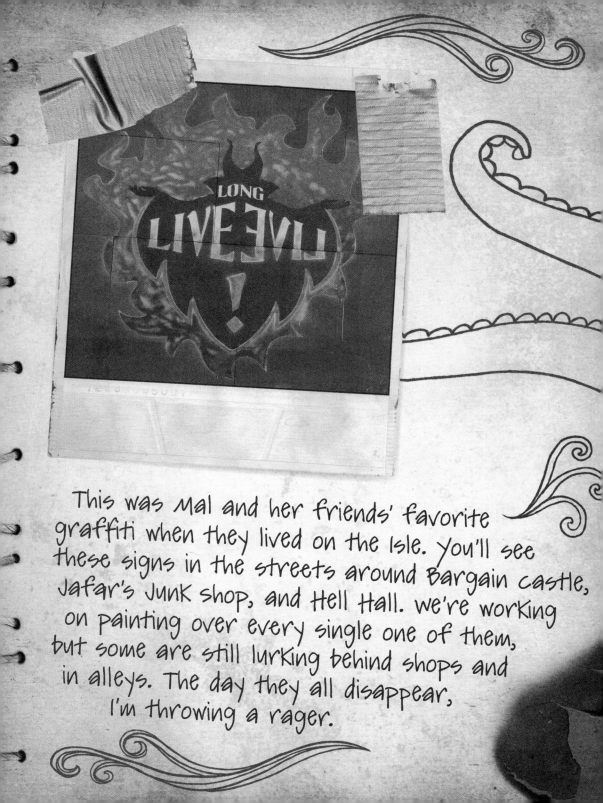

This was Mal and her friends' favorite graffiti when they lived on the Isle. You'll see these signs in the streets around Bargain castle, Jafar's Junk shop, and Hell Hall. We're working on painting over every single one of them, but some are still lurking behind shops and in alleys. The day they all disappear, I'm throwing a rager.

DOWN WITH AURADON!

I don't think there's a kid on the Isle who hasn't spray-painted this before. You'll see them all over, from coast to coast. We might not all get along, but we can all agree on one thing: Auradon deserves whatever it gets.

Ugh. Another one of Mal's old tags. Pretty funny now that she's practically a princess, huh? Wonder what King Ben would think of it . . .

We Ride With the Tide

This will always be my favorite thing to see in some back alley or painted on a brick wall. This one is all about me and my pirate posse. <u>Lost Revenge</u> represent!

'TIS INDEED. I'VE PUT UP A BUNCH OF THESE AROUND THE WHARF. AS SOON AS PEOPLE SET FOOT ON OUR STREETS, THEY NEED TO KNOW WHO THEY'RE DEALING WITH.

TROUBLE IS HERE

—WAYS TO **NOT** — BE A (TRAITOR) LIKE MAL!

1 Don't abandon your Isle people.

2 Don't become Auradon royalty.

3 Don't forget about your own suffering.

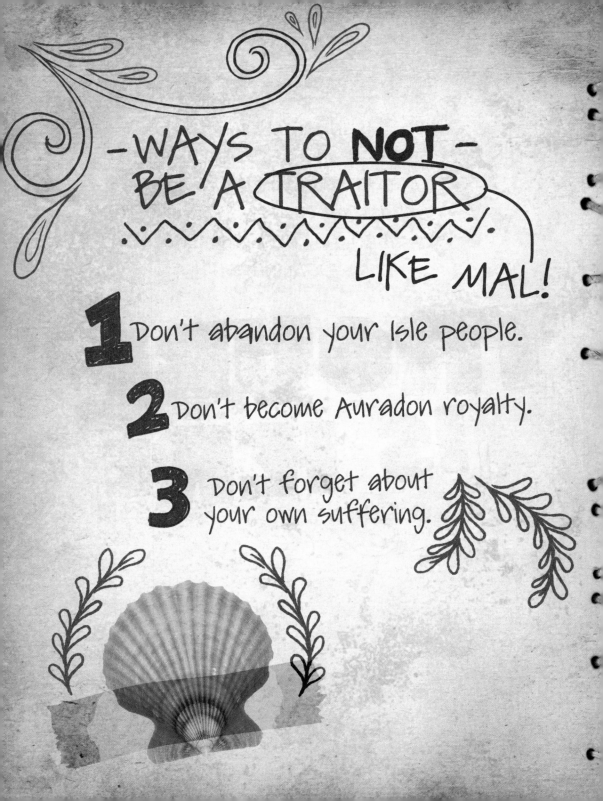

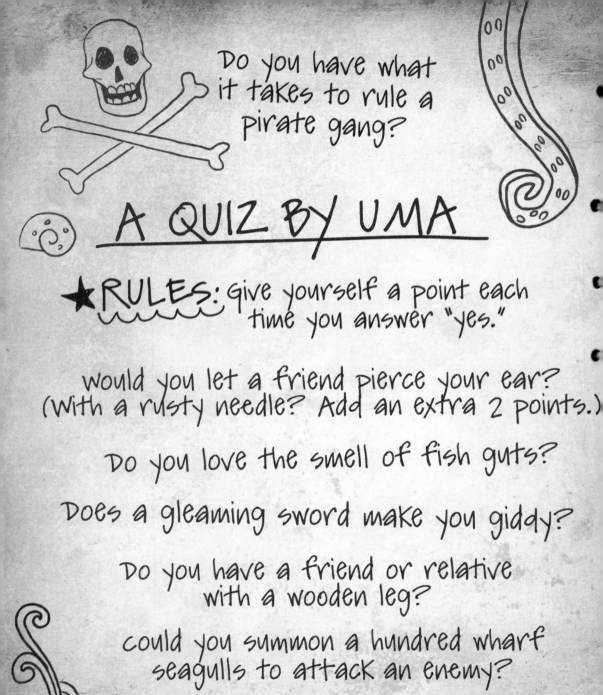

Do you have what it takes to rule a pirate gang?

A QUIZ BY UMA

★RULES: Give yourself a point each time you answer "yes."

Would you let a friend pierce your ear? (With a rusty needle? Add an extra 2 points.)

Do you love the smell of fish guts?

Does a gleaming sword make you giddy?

Do you have a friend or relative with a wooden leg?

Could you summon a hundred wharf seagulls to attack an enemy?

Does your hair look amazing when you use sea spray to style it?

Have you ever dated someone with an eye patch?

Does your best friend have a hook for a hand?

Have you ever wrestled a shark and lived to tell the story?

Can you untangle yourself from a fishing net in under thirty seconds?

Do you crave seaweed soda and dried crab slab after a good duel?

SCORING:

If you scored 10 points or more, you're fit to rule a gang of grungy pirates. If you scored 9 points or under, don't quit your day job!

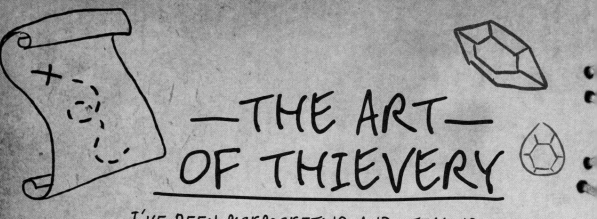

—THE ART—
OF THIEVERY

I'VE BEEN PICKPOCKETING AND STEALING FOR
QUITE A LONG TIME—SO LONG THAT IT'S BECOME AN
ART FORM. TAKE JAFAR'S JUNK SHOP, FOR EXAMPLE. I'VE
BEEN STEALING FROM THAT OLD GEEZER FOR ALMOST
A DECADE AND HE STILL HASN'T ACCUSED ME. LAST I
HEARD, HE THOUGHT IT WAS SAMMY SMEE (HAD THE
POOR BUGGER TIED UP FOR HOURS, HOPING HE'D CONFESS).

Now, I'd never tell anyone to nick something. . . . But if you find yourself in the position to "relieve someone of their possessions," you should keep these tips in mind:

1) Wear a big long coat, the bigger the better. Use one with a lot of pockets you can hide things in. (I even have secret pockets in mine.)

2) Choose things they won't miss. Jafar has his favorite pieces in his junk shop. There's a broken statue of Iago and a copper tea set he polishes daily. I wouldn't take those, because he'd notice they were gone right away. Instead, I pick things on lower shelves that I can resell.

3) Smaller items are less likely to be missed. I stole all the charms for Uma's bracelets and a bunch of the ones she put on her boots, too.

4) Buy something every now and then. I started doing this to throw off the scent, and it's worked. Jafar thinks I'm a paying customer.

After Mal left for Auradon and Maleficent was turned into the sniveling little lizard that she is, Bargain Castle was empty for a while. It sat right in the middle of the town square, the windows dark, just begging for people to raid it. Cobwebs piled up in every nook and cranny, and rats took over the place. So when a bunch of goblins broke down the door to loot it, my crew and I couldn't resist.

Apparently, Maleficent thought her refrigerator was a safe, because that's where I found all the best stuff. I fought a pack of goblins for an emerald necklace. There were leather-bound books filled with different spells, but they got torn apart in the chaos. I managed to get a cloak and shawl from one of her closets.

You've got to move fast. In a competitive situation like that, every second counts. I left the icebox to the goblins and went straight for Maleficent's closet. Found some raven feather boas that I sold in an alley for a handful of jewels, and a nice set of quills in her office that went for some gold coin. Wish we could've gotten into Mal's room, but there was a huge lock and chain on the door. No time to pick it . . .

All I got was a bite mark on my arm and a black eye. By the time the goblins stopped attacking me, everything was gone.

When it comes to thieving, there are big jobs and small jobs. The biggest job I ever did was nicking Cruella De Vil's red car. I'd had my sights set on it for months. She keeps it in the garage of Hell Hall, with about a hundred locks and chains on the door. I had to wait for the perfect moment to strike. . . . I went in alone, not wanting to risk anyone blowing it for me.

That kind of hurts my feelings. You think I would've blown it for you?

YES.

I didn't get there until after midnight, when the streets around Hell Hall were dark. I'd brought all my best lock-picking tools. There must've been two dozen locks of all sizes. I went through them one by one, pulling off the chains, too, until I finally got the door free.

I only lifted it a few feet because I didn't want to make any noise. Then I rolled underneath and climbed into the car. She'd left the keys in the ignition. (How daft was that?) As soon as I was sure I'd be able to start it, I rolled the garage door up the rest of the way, turned the engine on, and peeled out, not looking back.

My plan was to break down the car and sell the parts on the Isle black market, making a pretty profit. But it was hard to even go a few blocks without people noticing me. Everyone on the Isle knows Cruella's car, and a few people started hooting and shouting that someone had taken it. I parked it in an alley and ran before anyone could find her and tell her. Maybe it was a lot of effort for just a joyride and bragging rights, but I still think it was worth it.

STINK BOMB RECIPE

These are good old-fashioned fun. Throw them at your enemies or use them as a distraction while you're stealing some loot. Just be careful—the smell doesn't come off for weeks.

YOU'LL NEED:

2 cups goblin snot

1 teaspoon crushed newt spleen

1/2 cup curdled milk

2 teaspoons slug slime, divided

4 empty eggshells (both halves)

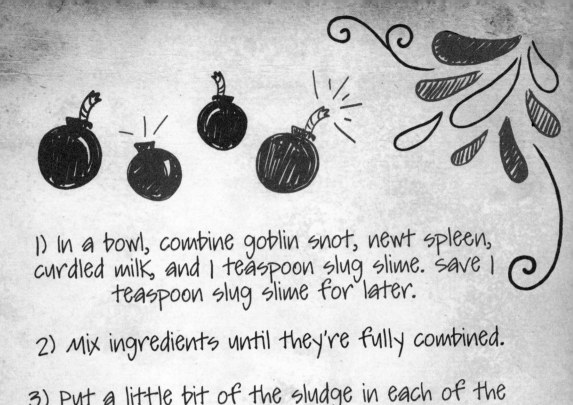

1) In a bowl, combine goblin snot, newt spleen, curdled milk, and 1 teaspoon slug slime. Save 1 teaspoon slug slime for later.

2) Mix ingredients until they're fully combined.

3) Put a little bit of the sludge in each of the eggshells, saving the matching halves.

4) Use the extra slug slime to glue the matching halves together.

5) Let the slime dry for at least a day before using. (Wait three days to get the smelliest stink bombs.)

VENGEANCE

There was this cool old broken photo booth outside Frollo's creperie that someone jury-rigged to get it to work for a little while.

I THINK IT WAS CARLOS. THAT LITTLE RUNT IS GOOD FOR SOME THINGS, I GUESS.

Everyone loved it, but of course no one here knows how to have nice things, so it got broken within a day or two.

The goblins did a number on it.

Anyway, I saved these photos of us. we're a pretty <u>fierce-looking</u> crew!!

DOING THE TIME FOR CRIME

There's no "official" punishment, no way of getting in trouble on the Isle of the Lost. we don't have judges or juries or anything like that. King Ben can say the Isle is under his rule, but it's not like he's prowling the streets looking out for people stealing cars or graffiting walls. The only thing a villain has to worry about is revenge. It's real, and if you're on the receiving end of it, it can make life on the Isle impossible.

CRUELLA DE VIL EVENTUALLY DID FIND OUT I NICKED HER CAR. ONE OF THE TWITS WHO SAW ME DRIVE OFF MUST HAVE TOLD HER WHAT HAD HAPPENED. I'D HEARD RUMORS SHE WAS AFTER ME, THAT SHE WAS JUST LYING IN WAIT, BUT WHENEVER I SAW HER IN THE MARKET SHE SMILED HER WICKED SMILE AND WENT ON HER WAY. I'D STARTED TO THINK SHE'D FORGOTTEN ALL ABOUT IT. . . .

IT WENT DOWN ONE NIGHT WHEN I WAS WALKING HOME FROM THE WHARF. THE STREETS WERE DARK AND I GOT A FUNNY FEELING. SOMETHING WASN'T RIGHT. I TURNED AROUND AND SAW TWO FIGURES IN THE ALLEY BEHIND ME. I STARTED TO RUN, BUT THEY CAUGHT ME. IT WAS JASPER AND HORACE, CRUELLA'S EVIL HENCHMEN, AND THEY WERE IMPOSSIBLE TO FIGHT OFF. THEY DRAGGED ME DOWN TO THE TOWN SQUARE AND PUT ME IN THE STOCKS, THAT WEIRD WOODEN THING THAT LOCKS YOUR HEAD AND HANDS IN PLACE. I STAYED THERE FOR TWO DAYS UNTIL MY DAD GOT CRUELLA TO AGREE TO RELEASE ME.

I believe in revenge for revenge. If Cruella locked me in the stocks for two days, I'd steal something from her she couldn't get back. Maybe I'd take some of those fur coats, or I'd capture Jasper and Horace and keep them prisoner on the <u>Lost Revenge</u>. An eye for an eye for an eye for an eye . . .

GOTTA KEEP THE CYCLE GOING, YA KNOW?

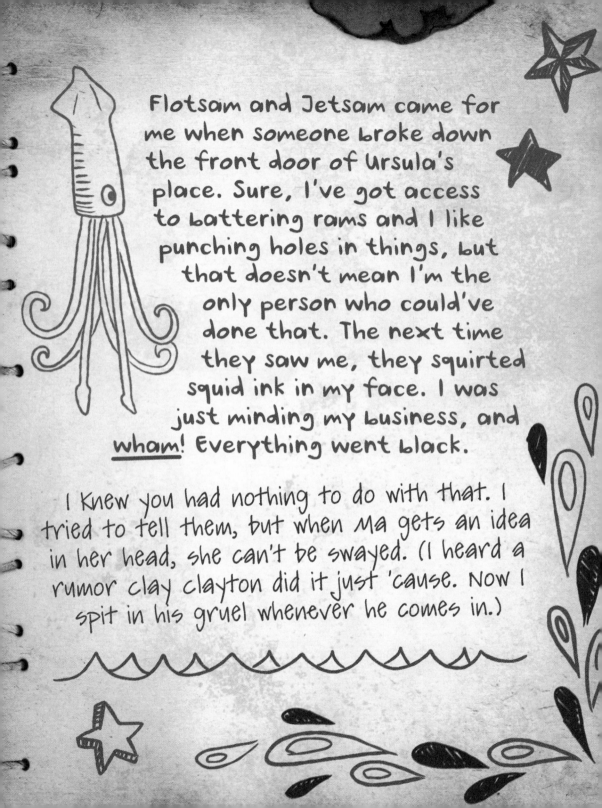

Flotsam and Jetsam came for me when someone broke down the front door of Ursula's place. Sure, I've got access to battering rams and I like punching holes in things, but that doesn't mean I'm the only person who could've done that. The next time they saw me, they squirted squid ink in my face. I was just minding my business, and __wham!__ Everything went black.

I knew you had nothing to do with that. I tried to tell them, but when Ma gets an idea in her head, she can't be swayed. (I heard a rumor Clay Clayton did it just 'cause. Now I spit in his gruel whenever he comes in.)

A VILLAIN'S TURF

winning the <u>Lost Revenge</u> from captain Hook was one of the best things that's ever happened to me. I entered a boat race against a whole slew of goblins, but I was the only one who made it across the finish line. Those first days when we could sail the ship out on the water, the wind in my braids . . . Those were the best. It was the closest thing I've known to freedom.

The ship was ruined in a storm when Harry, Gil, and I were trying to get King Triton's trident. Now it's busted. Holes in the sides, a cracked mast. It's beyond repair, permanently docked in the harbor, but that doesn't matter; I still love every inch of it. Because every inch of it is mine.

My whole life, I never had a place to call my own. All those days spent working at Ma's restaurant, serving up gruel and scrubbing the floors, and I've never gotten paid a coin. My room in our sea cave only has a few things in it, because Ma's always yelling at me to keep it clean. Being on the <u>Lost Revenge</u> isn't like that at all.

I used to just hang out in the crow's nest by myself, watching the wharf and the bustling port, the guys selling eels' heads and clams. I felt like a queen in her castle.

I spray-painted this myself.

The plank is perfect for holding hostages. Keep their hands and feet tied. Just one shove and they're shark bait.

This was an extra strand of lights Ma had left over from the chip shop. Gil strung them up for me. They're one of my favorite parts of the ship.

Took me five hours to get all the bulbs working.

I climb these ropes to get a better vantage point.

My very own room is the captain's quarters, with no one to tell me to clean it. This bed is the coziest place I've ever slept.

There is also the ship's "loo," as Harry calls it. That's just a British term for bathroom. It has a giant cracked mirror where I can do my hair and a tub big enough for a warm bath.

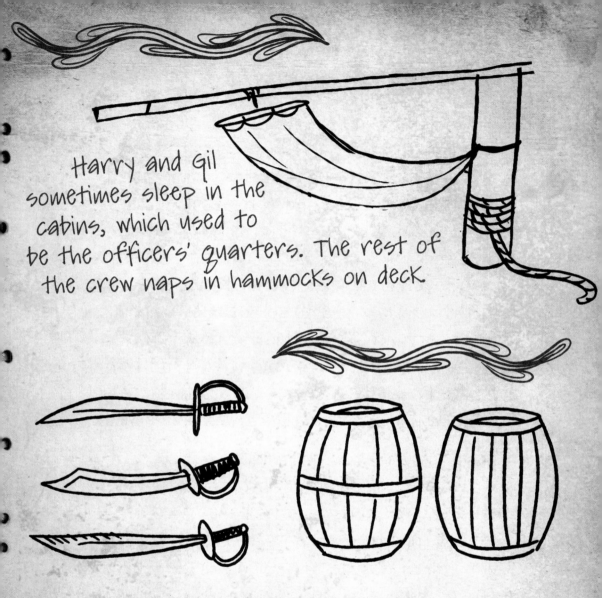

Harry and Gil sometimes sleep in the cabins, which used to be the officers' quarters. The rest of the crew naps in hammocks on deck.

We keep all our most valuable supplies on board. Swords, sails, and some of the canned goods we've gotten from the Auradon shipments. I don't feel weird telling you this (whoever you are) because you found my book here, hidden behind those wooden barrels. I had hoped only someone stealthy and clever would discover it. . . .

Any pirate who's worth her salt needs a fierce pirate crew. I knew that, but it was still hard at first—never letting your guard down, always making sure you commanded respect. I didn't realize being a leader was so much work. One time, when my crew had just come together, I made the mistake of going to the market alone to collect some unpaid debts. A bunch of ruffians stole a bag of rubies, my sword, and even my favorite belt buckle. I came back empty-handed and was foolish enough to tell my crew what happened.

Now I never show any weakness. I never want to lose my crew's respect. I like to have at least two scallywags back me up on the wharf, and at least five during a sword fight. Harry and Gil have been my right-hand men for ages now, and I know they're looking out for me, no matter what. But it's not easy keeping the boys in line. . . .

Never show Weakness!

RULING YOUR PIRATE CREW

- Make them call you by your name. I like to have them chant "Uma" to boost my confidence before a fight.

- Every pirate needs to earn their keep. Someone's gotta swab the deck.

  THANK THE DEVIL IT ISN'T ME.

  Or me.

- Keep your secrets. Mistakes or missteps should never be shared. Make them think you're perfect. (You are.)

- Every queen needs a throne. I have a special chair in the chip shop that only I'm allowed to sit in. It's decorated with different sea treasures my crew's collected over the years. The boys hoist me up so everyone can worship me.

- Never let them know where they stand. Your pirates should be working day and night to impress you.

  EVEN ME?

  I guess you're the exception. You know you're my second-in-command.

- Fear is your friend. Make sure they don't know what you're capable of. As far as they know, anyone can become shark bait at any moment.

LOST REVENGE
CHORE SHEET

CAPTAIN: UMA, DAUGHTER OF URSULA

FIRST MATE: HARRY HOOK

DOLE OUT PUNISHMENTS: HARRY ✓

MOP THE DECK: DESIREE ✓

SHARPEN THE SWORDS: BONNY ✓

CARRY SHIPMENTS TO/FROM WHARF: GIL ✓

FILL THE CHUM BUCKETS: GONZO ✓

STOCK THE PANTRY: GONZO ✓

MAN THE CANNONS: JONAS ✓

KEEP LOOKOUT: GIL ✓

So I didn't get my hook the old-fashioned way, by losing my hand. There was no monstrous crocodile fight. It wasn't smashed under a falling boulder. Dad gave me this one to wear with my pirate outfit, and I reckon it's just as menacing. When I hold up my hook, even the fiercest villains take a few steps back. But it's got other uses, too. . . .

HOW TO WIELD A HOOK

—Just set it on the counter when you're buying something at the Slop Shop. Nine times out of ten, the muffin's free.

— Hold it up if someone threatens you. This'll stop a fight before it starts.

— Use it to carve your initials into the ship's deck.

Not on my watch.

— Hook some chains or ropes for easy transport.

— Get the shrimp shells out from between those back molars. You'll never need a toothpick again.

I use fish bones as toothpicks.

— Run it along a metal table to get the room's attention.

I hate when you do that. It makes me want to sic the sharks on you.

SHARK SNACKS

After so many years on shark swim Team, I Know the sharks around the Isle really well. Fang and Bully are the ones I usually swim with, and crusher and Meathead are really popular with the rest of the team. But there are dozens of others that hang out in the waters around the wharf. The sharks by the <u>Lost Revenge</u> are the meanest and wildest.

There are at least ten of them, and sometimes it seems like they're always hungry, Knocking into the boat and begging for food. I've finally learned what they like and don't like, and what will make them madder than Madam Mim.

BEST THINGS TO FEED SHARKS:

HOSTAGES
(this is always their favorite, but a plump, terrified hostage is hard to come by)

FISH GUTS
SEVERED EEL HEADS
ROTTEN EGGS

WORST THINGS TO FEED SHARKS

OLD BOOTS
(WARNING: Do not test this. Bartholomew, the biggest and angriest shark, rammed a hole in the ship once after tasting Gil's shoe.)

TRASH
ANYTHING SWEET
(old candies, cookies, cinnamon buns)

BLOOD
(It just makes them crazy but doesn't stop their hunger.)

Sword fighting is about getting your enemy to the point where they have to give up. As soon as they know they're going to lose, they'll say and do whatever you want them to. I've been in dozens of duels over the years, and I've never shed a drop of blood. A good swordsman doesn't have to.

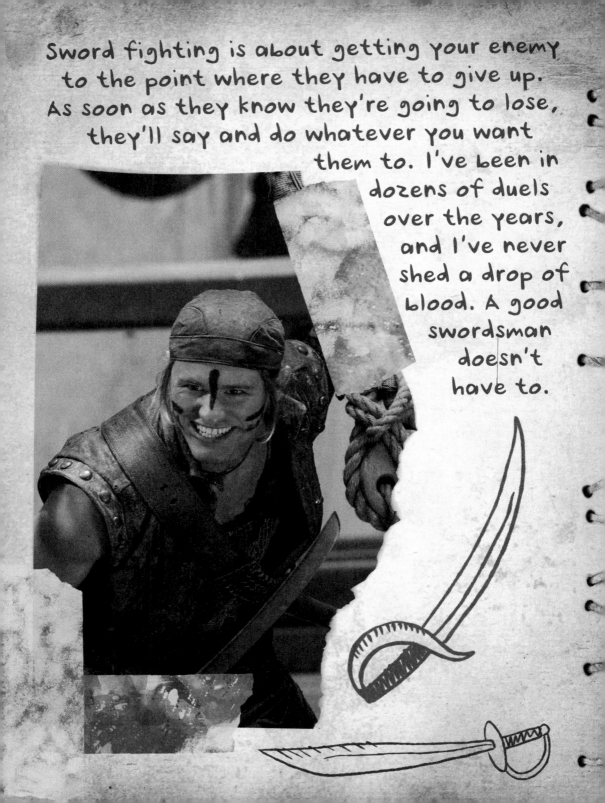

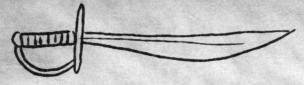

SWORD FIGHTING 101

-Know your surroundings. Can you trap your enemy? Pin them against a wall? Learn how to use where you are to your advantage.

- Have your sword out before you approach.

— Be light on your feet.

-Face away from the sun whenever you can. Even the tiniest bit peeking through the smog and clouds can be blinding.

-Keep your balance. Make sure there's nothing you might trip on.

-Have your elbows bent close to your body.

- Never turn your back on your enemy.

-Keep your empty hand out of the way.

-Stay calm and confident. Try to intimidate your opponent into giving up.

ISLE-ING OUT

DEFINITION: Going crazy or getting wild, Isle-style. Doing something you shouldn't be doing.

GETTING -INTO- TROUBLE

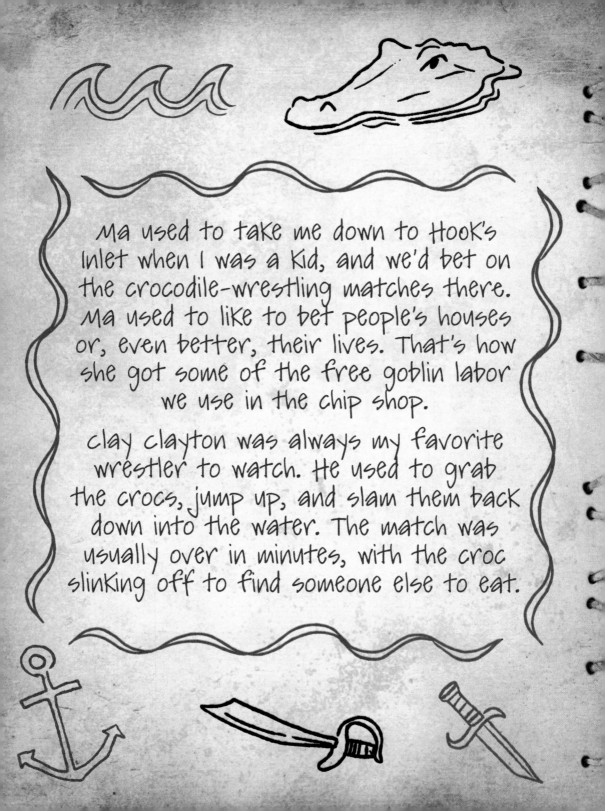

Ma used to take me down to Hook's Inlet when I was a Kid, and we'd bet on the crocodile-wrestling matches there. Ma used to like to bet people's houses or, even better, their lives. That's how she got some of the free goblin labor we use in the chip shop.

Clay Clayton was always my favorite wrestler to watch. He used to grab the crocs, jump up, and slam them back down into the water. The match was usually over in minutes, with the croc slinking off to find someone else to eat.

I'VE PINNED MY FAIR SHARE OF CROCS AFTER SCHOOL IN CROC WRESTLING CLUB, BUT THE WRESTLERS BY THE INLET ARE PROFESSIONALS. IF YOU'RE PLACING BETS WITH SAMMY SMEE, IT'S SAFEST TO GO WITH MY SISTER HARRIET OR WITH SCAR OR CLAYTON. THEY'RE AS CLOSE TO A SURE THING AS YOU CAN GET. THESE ARE SOME OF THE OTHER (LESS SUCCESSFUL) MATCHES I'VE SEEN:

GASTON vs. A TEN-FOOT CROCODILE
(SORRY, GIL, IT'S TRUE)

GASTON GOT BIT ON THE TOE IN THE FIRST TWO MINUTES AND STARTED SCREAMING.

FLOTSAM AND JETSAM
vs.
TWO BABY CROCODILES

THEY WERE WINNING FOR A WHILE, BUT THEN JETSAM TURNED HIS BACK ON THE CROCS. THEY QUICKLY TOOK HIM DOWN.

JADE vs. A SIX-FOOT CROCODILE
JADE, JAY'S COUSIN, TRIED TO FIGHT THE CROC UNDERWATER. HUGE MISTAKE. SHE ALMOST DROWNED.

Some days the smog on the Isle is so thick it chokes you. I'll be sitting in the crow's nest on the <u>Lost Revenge</u>, staring off at the mainland, thinking there must be more than this. Am I really supposed to spend my whole life here, trapped on the Isle of the Lost, ruling these twits?
(offense, guys. Take it.)

COME ON, CAPTAIN, ARE WE REALLY THAT BAD?

If you've spent a lot of time on the Isle, you've thought about what it would be like to get off it. To live somewhere—anywhere—else. Because when you're eating rock-hard bread for the third day in a row, and you haven't seen the sun in weeks, and you're walking down the same street for the thousandth time, seeing all the same faces, it can start to feel a little claustrophobic. Honestly, part of me is always thinking about . . .

ESCAPING

THE ISLE

TRAITORS IN TIARAS

I'll never forget the day Mal and her friends left for Auradon. They were pretending to be all annoyed that King Ben had summoned them and they had to leave. They were complaining about it nonstop, but I knew they had to be at least a little bit excited. Who HASN'T dreamt of getting out of this place?

Afterward, rumors spread through the streets like Shere Khan's snakes. Everyone kept saying that Mal was too bad to go to Auradon. They said she'd overturn Belle and Beast's rule and free everyone on the Isle of the Lost. They were sure that, before long, she'd return, and she'd help all of us escape. But I knew the truth. I never thought she'd be anything less than the traitor she became. Because when you get the chance to leave the Isle of the Lost, most people don't look back. There's just no reason to.

I guess I still wonder about that day, though. . . . What did Mal have that I didn't? What was so different about her and her friends? I'd worked so hard at Ma's shop, sweeping floors and serving gruel and never once complaining. Wasn't that worth something? Why didn't Ben pick me? Don't I deserve a better life?

The answer is yes. I definitely do . . . and so do you.

TRAITOR

WORST THINGS ABOUT
BEING TRAPPED ON THE ISLE

- Only one TV station
- stale, rotten leftover food
- Limited supplies
- smog and cloud cover
- Everyone's in a bad mood all the time.
- No wi-fi or cell service. NEED I SAY MORE?!?

One of the meanest things Belle and Beast do is air Auradon-sponsored propaganda (excuse me, "TV programming"). All day every day our TVs show hours and hours of King Ben and Mal! Teatime with Jasmine and Aladdin! An afternoon press conference to talk about nothing! Mal sneezed, did you villains hear yet?!? Can you believe it?!?

YUCK.

It wasn't always that way. When Harry, Gil, and I were kids there was this local TV station that broadcast to all the villains on the Isle. It was hours of wicked, wacky television. Sure, you had to hit the TV a few times to get the reception working, but I could've watched it all day. Sometimes I did.

When I was in middle school, Belle and Beast ruled against it, and <u>poof!</u> The channel was gone.

TELEVISION GUIDE

TIME ▶ CHANNEL ▼	5:30PM	6:00PM	6:30PM	7:00PM
AAC	TODDLERS WITHOUT TIARAS		AURADON'S CLASSIEST HOME VIDEOS	
ABS	BIG BLING THEORY	AURADON NINJA WARRIOR		BIG BLING THEORY
NAC	THE PRINCE IS RIGHT		HOW I MET YOUR FAIRY GODMOTHER	
WDA	TRADING CARPETS		PALACES AND CORONATIONS	
BIPPITY!	REAL PRINCESSES OF CHARMINGSVILLE		REAL PRINCESSES OF CHARMINGSVILL	
MAGIC NETWORK	STRANGER THINGAMABOBS	GET DOWN WITH THE BALLGOWN	*stepsister, stepsister +*	
KINDNESS	MY FAIRY LADY	MY FAIRY LADY	*say yes to the hex*	
villain BROADCASTING SYSTEM	~~THE ZOUNG AND THE CROWNLESS~~ *Pretty Little Lairs*		~~○○○○~~	
COURTESY CENTRAL	LITTLE DWARFS, BIG GIANTS		LITTLE DWARFS, BIG GIAN	
GOOD DEEDS	THE GREAT AURADON BAKE OFF		THE GREAT AURADON BA	
NATIONAL ENCHANTMENT	CHIPPED	TRADING CARPETS	CHIPPED	
FAIRY PLANET	AURORA THE EXPLORER		AURORA THE EXPLO	

Best shows on EVIL ISLE, our old TV station

Skin Deep with Mother Gothel

she might be wrinkled as a raisin now that she doesn't have her magic flower, but she still knows a lot about beauty routines. she was the one who taught me to put egg whites on my face to keep my skin shiny and smooth.

JUDGE FROLLO

This one was the best. villains would drag in someone they wanted to exact revenge on, and Judge Frollo would rule how and when they could do it. sometimes he'd go on these long, rambling tirades to make them feel stupid. Harry and I used to laugh and laugh watching it.

Smee took a camera down to Hook's Inlet and kept it on the crocs for hours. It was pretty boring, but he said some weird, interesting stuff occasionally, and every now and then a croc would come out of the water. I thought it was pretty calming.

WHARF WATCH

Cruella De Vil's $ Coat Club

I hate to admit it, but I liked watching Cruella's hour-long sales special. She'd model different coats and try to get villains to call in and buy them. She even let you pay in ten easy installments, so you only had to put out a little coin at a time.

FEELING HAPPY?
WE CAN HELP.

CALL THE HAPPINESS PREVENTION HOTLINE.

(555) JOY-FULL

I've never had problems with this on the Isle. . . . It's not a happy place.

THINGS I'D MISS ABOUT THE ISLE

- My pirate crew
- The <u>Lost Revenge</u>
- Impromptu sword fights
- Impromptu dance parties
- Donuts and burnt coffee at The slop shop
- Being carried around on my seashell throne
- Hearing my crew chant my name
- Crepes . . . I love Frollo's crepes.
- Being universally feared
- Feeling the cool wharf winds in my hair
- The smell of the ocean in the morning

- Cornelius and Greta
(I tear up just thinking of them.)

THINGS I WOULDN'T MISS ABOUT THE ISLE

- working long hours at the chip shop
- Ma yelling at me
- Feeling hopeless, like I have no future
- Having to make all my clothes by hand
- How angry everyone is here
- getting sick from spoiled food
- Always having to watch your back

HOW TO ESCAPE THE ISLE OF THE LOST

1) Think, think, and rethink everything. What connections do you have that others don't? Is there anyone you can use to get off the Isle? Is there a perfect time to leave? Will you take anyone with you? I thought about leaving for years before I actually did anything about it.

2) Make a plan. You should plot out your escape down to the minute, then be ready to improvise some things if you have to.

3) Do your research. Where are you headed? What do people wear there? How do they talk? What do they eat? You'll want to blend in as much as possible, so make sure you know your future surroundings.

4) Consider your supplies. You'll want to take things with you, sure, but not all Isle goods can be used on the mainland. Toss the gold teeth in favor of some canned lima beans, which you can eat in a pinch. (Just make sure to bring a can opener, too.)

5) Don't say your goodbyes. The fewer people who know you're leaving, the better. You don't want anyone messing up the plan or, worse, trying to stop you.

ONE LAST HURRAH

I've been saving all my tips from the chip shop in a giant barrel behind my bed. I have piles of gold teeth, silver buttons, and metal chains that are just burning a hole in the floor. You see, where I'm headed, you can't just throw down a handful of glass eyes when you want to buy something. This currency only works on the Isle. So I decided to take my crew out for one last hurrah. . . .

Tonight we went to Shan-Yu's Dim Sum. I didn't mention it before, because honestly, most people on the Isle can't afford it, and despite my reputation, I don't like making people feel bad if I don't have to. The tables are covered in this beautiful red cloth and he somehow finds all the best dishes in the shipments from Auradon. There are tiny lanterns hanging from the ceiling and the silver is so shiny you can see your reflection in it. And the food . . . it's better than I imagined.

My crew and I have a big day tomorrow, and everyone's excited. We toasted and cheered and laughed at Gil. (It's always fun to laugh at Gil.) Even though Shan-Yu always seems angry when I see him in the street, he was in a great mood tonight, and he smiled and laughed with us. We ate until our stomachs were so full they hurt. I saved the menu as a souvenir—I want to remember this night forever.

SHAN-YU'S DIM SUM

		QUANTITY
STEAMED BUNS	✗	2
SOUR SOUP DUMPLINGS	✗	3
DEEP-FRIED BEAN DUMPLINGS		
ROTTEN EGG DROP SOUP MY FAVORITE!	✗	2
CHICKEN NOODLE SOUP	✗	1
STEAMED BEEF BALL		
CHIVES & SHRIMP CAKES		
SWEET & SOUR FISH		
CRAB PINCERS THE BEST!!	✗	2
STICKY RICE WITH LOTUS		
& CREAM BUN		
RIBS		
ROLL WITH SHRIMP		

URSULA'S FISH & CHIPS

You'll take it how I make it!

WEEK 212

Name **UMA, Daughter of Ursula**

AGE: NOTHING/HOUR

DAY	IN	OUT
MON	SUNRISE	SUNSET
TUES	SUNRISE	SUNSET
WED	SUNRISE	SUNSET
THUR	SUNRISE	SUNSET
FRI	SUNRISE	SUNSET
SAT	SUNRISE	SUNSET
SUN	OFF	OFF
TOTAL		

Signed *Ursula*

I WON'T BE NEEDING THIS ANYMORE.

I've had my own crazy attempts to get through the barrier over the years, but they were nothing compared to some of the stuff I've seen on the wharf. I've been thinking carefully about getting off the Isle, and I've come up with the perfect plan, because so many villains have really flubbed it up. Make sure you do your research before you decide how you'll escape. (Hopefully, by now you've heard all about how I did it.)

HERE ARE THE <u>WORST</u> OF THE <u>WORST</u> BARRIER FAILS

That time smee threw a bunch of rotten meat at the barrier, hoping the crocodiles would chew through it.

That time Gaston and Gaston Jr. used one of their battering rams on it. It got wet and slipped from their hands, pinning Gaston Jr. underwater. Gaston was able to save him, but one of Gaston Jr.'s legs was broken.

That time Evil Queen tried to set the barrier on fire. she put this weird solution on it and lit it up, but it just caused a bright flash. It didn't do anything except burn her eyebrows and eyelashes off.

That time cruella drove over the bridge going sixty miles an hour and crashed into the barrier. Her hood crunched like an accordion. It took ages for Jasper and Horace to fix it.

I've stared out the from the
crow's nest at Auradon so many
times. It was always off in the
distance, taunting us. Of course
I've never seen it IRL. Just photos,
like the one on this this one that
washed up in a bag of trash.

<u>HOME</u> <u>WICKED</u> <u>HOME</u>

There are things I'll miss about the Isle of the Lost—there really are. The smell of the wharf winds on a cool, crisp day. The taste of a seaweed smoothie. Laughing with Harry about some stupid, silly thing Gil said. Dancing on the deck of the <u>Lost Revenge</u>, my whole pirate crew behind me.

This place made me who I am. I can get thousands of miles away from it, but it'll always be part of me, no matter what. I couldn't change that even if I wanted to.

Now time is running out. I'm going to leave the Isle behind soon. Just do me a favor, will you? Take care of this place for me. You never know when I might be back. . . .

These next pages are for your own notes on how to survive and thrive in a terrible place. Feel free to add any sneaky tricks or wretched ideas.

GET WICKED WITH IT!!

—UMA

—HARRY

—Gil

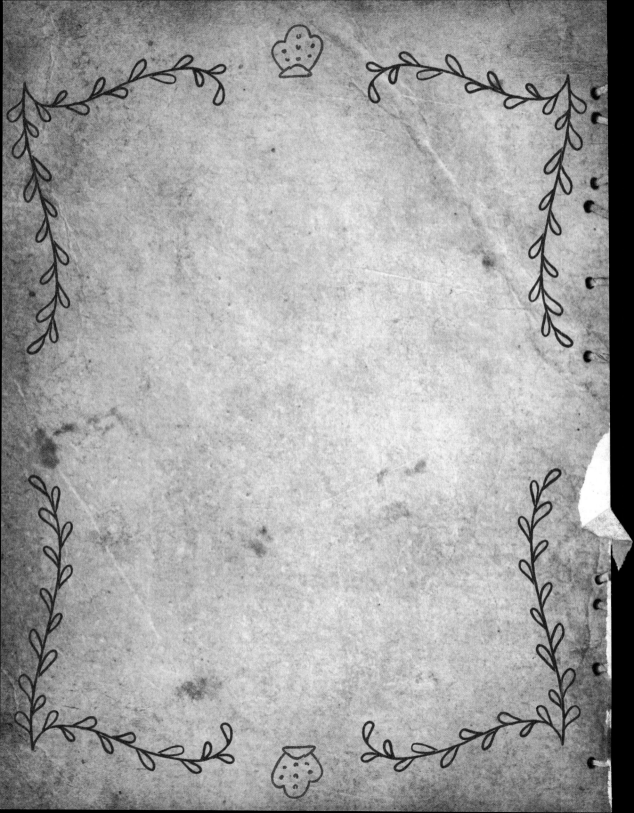